Another FIFTH OF JULY

Surfside Beach Series

Another Fifth of July

KELLY CAPRIOTTI BURTON

First Printing, 2024

This is a work of fiction. Names, characters, organizations, places, events, and incidents are either products of the author's imagination or are used fictitiously.

Published by Kell of a Story
Cover design & back cover photo by Kelly Capriotti Burton
Author photo by Amy Jane Photography

ISBN: 978-1-7361174-9-1

kellofastory.com
Surfside Beach, South Carolina

 DEDICATION

To my sister Shannon Marie, for the trustworthy, eternal, mostly metaphorical presence of 162.50.

Jessie

"Jess. Wake up. You're missing the best part."

"What? Oh, good grief." I hadn't wanted to fall asleep, but riding shotgun through the winding mountain roads, lined by lush trees and views of the Blue Ridge mountains, had done me in.

Paul didn't try to hide his amusement. I had made quite the overture that morning about staying awake to keep him company. We were both already exhausted from life's latest chaotic events: helping Sam and Abby make the move that had spurred the need for this trip, transitioning the ownership of my tea room business to my sister Maggie, assisting my youngest daughter Brittney in the purchase of her first home, welcoming Paul's youngest, Katy, back to living at the beach full time after her years of pretending to be the black sheep up in Wilmington, and trying to look cool as I searched once again for what our new normal was going to look like.

I hated that phrase.

Just over two years ago, you could have knocked me over with a feather had I caught a glimpse into my current life. Both my sons living out of state would have been unthinkable. Now Sam, the oldest, would soon live here, in beautiful Union County, Georgia, with his wife Abby and their two youngest children, Summer and Jacob. My youngest son David, the de facto baby of our blended brood, had been living in Knoxville, Tennessee and visited… sometimes. It could never be enough, truth be told. The fact that I was matriarch of a blended brood, that my husband of thirty-six years had passed suddenly and tragically alongside Paul's wife in a car accident, that grief and friendship and complicated intimacy had mingled together and here we were, married, all of those things were my surreality. I guess I could still be knocked over with a feather.

"It will be nice to have this cabin all to ourselves," I offered lamely. Paul and I *lived* by ourselves, as folks in their sixties were wont to do. But we had purchased a beach cottage with what our grandkids called a secret passage way and what our more wayward kids, nieces, and sometimes, my sister, referred to as "second home." It was, in actuality, an attached but separate apartment that I had made all too welcoming and that Paul wanted to fill with concrete after a year of revolving housemates.

And continuing that script, my husband gave a sardonic little laugh, never taking his eyes from the curvy road before us. "You know that Summer and Jacob are going to want to stay with us."

I looked out my window, pondering my response. I hadn't spent much time in the mountains through the years. When Randall and I first moved from the suburbs of Chicago to coastal South Carolina, our parents had still been alive, and we had made the trek back and forth several times a year. It was a fourteen-hour drive without any stops, and the mountains were a short part of it, but always my favorite. Randall had laughed at me every time I wondered out loud who had conceived the idea of putting roads through them, and how in God's name had they done it? I possessed a poet's soul, not an engineer's brain. I still could not conceive how anyone cut and paved all those pathways through miles and miles of ancient rock.

Stubbornness was no match for someone with a dream, I guess.

I looked back at Paul, noticing the tired slump in his shoulders, and knew what to say and more importantly, what to do. "Of course they'll want to sleep over," I said. "We're here for three nights, so let's let them stay for one. Maybe two? I want to spend the time, but—"

We need a break, I finished silently.

We'd barely been married a year. No, we weren't newlyweds grasping to find our way in the world. We were battle-weary players in our own second act (some would say third, but I refused. People were living into their nineties plenty these days, which meant we could have a strong thirty years left). In the last thirteen months, we'd encountered a cancer diagnosis (mine), an angry daughter returning to town with no place to live (his), several visits from upheaval-causing siblings (mine), the birth of a new grandbaby (his), the selling off of a business (mine). We had both effectively re-retired again with that last decision, though

Paul was going to keep teaching his class at Coastal Carolina and we both wanted to keep writing. *(Keep? How about start again, Jess?)* But first, we were hanging here for a few days to help Sam and Abby find a place to live, and we'd return soon after to help with the move.

"We need a really long nap," Paul murmured. Then he sighed for the 800th time that day, but I wasn't worried about him being frustrated. I recognized the sigh. He was breathing out the stress of the last year, maybe to some degree the last two years. He was breathing out the exhaustion of balancing grief and excitement, guilt and love, aging and exuberance. We lived in the tenuous tension of it all, but maybe we were turning a corner into a steadier, calmer time. His sigh, I decided, was a holy exhale.

I managed to stay awake for the rest of the drive, which all told, was less than thirty minutes, but I was proud of me, nonetheless.

Guided by Airbnb's map, we pulled up an almost hidden gravel road and made a sharp right. There was a sign shaped like an owl and covered in mosaic tiles that announced we were at "Cabin Time." I felt my heart go pitter-pat. One of the first things I learned upon moving to the southeastern coast from the Midwest about a million years ago was that beach people love the mountains. It was a cliché I didn't mind holding true.

Paul was out of the Jeep and stretching before I even had my seatbelt off. I scanned the landscape, taking in the blue mountains in the distance, the old trees establishing a perimeter around the half acre of the property, the actual babbling brook I could hear through the closed windows, the gazebo that sat at its shore beckoning someone to come and read or chat or nap, and best of all, the cabin itself. There was a porch wrapping three sides and just like the description I had found, I could see the promised "whimsical touches" everywhere, lanterns of various sizes and signs with kitschy sayings and more mosaic art hanging down to cover the underbelly of the house. I counted thirteen rocking chairs of differing colors before I jumped out of the vehicle myself, anxious to see if the inside matched the outside.

Paul reached for my hand and smiled at me. "You love it already, don't you?" His eyes twinkled, and I felt a bit of immediate relief. Asking him to make this drive twice in a few weeks was a lot, but Sam and Abby moving away was even more life-altering, and Paul… It made me feel guilty to admit even to myself, but Paul would do just about anything for me. Knowing that, I tried not to ask for much. This would be my last bout of ridiculousness for a while, and we needed the time away anyway.

"I do," I answered, smiley wholly back at him. "Thank you for driving. Are you good?"

He nodded and clasped his hands back together, stretching his arms over his head. "It's a great drive once we're out of South Carolina." He was right. With the lack of any real highway leading to our beach, it took a very un-scenic forever to get out of our state. His arms went behind his hips, and he stretched his back every which way. "I wonder if there's a yoga studio in there. Or a chiropractor."

I gave him a secret smile that said, "Let's go see," and possibly implied, "Let's test the bed before Sam, et al. get here." He followed me in a way that suggested he understood both messages.

Twenty minutes later, I glanced quickly at my phone, tossed it on the little table next to the bed, and stood up to, well, find my shorts. Sam and Abby had gotten to town the day before and were staying at an inn about five miles away, but they were picking up our Walmart order of provisions and delivering them to us. Paul's only request for the two trips here was that we would stay in our own place.

"They're on the way," I announced.

"Of course they are," Paul said. Then he followed up with, "This bed will do."

I flopped back down next to him, pantless, rumpled, and smiling like the cat who got the canary. Except I didn't feel like the canary. I was just as satisfied and not ready to start the family part of the trip yet. I burrowed back into his chest and stared up at the wooden ceiling beams.

"You like the place alright?" he asked.

Without hesitation, I answered, "It's perfect. It's the exact description from the listing and exactly what I wanted it to be."

The window air unit was working full throttle, so I covered us with the airy white quilt, even though I knew we had to get ourselves together. Quilts are so quintessentially *cabin*. Everything about this place was quintessential cabin, from the layered linens to the clashing patterned textiles, the oiled wood walls and floors, the tiny tables with lamps in every nook and cranny, the mismatched chairs around the long wooden dining table, painted a faded yellow. Twenty minutes? It already felt like a home.

"I bet we won't be hearing any fireworks here tonight," Paul murmured. He ran his hand up and down my arm, barely touching me and giving me a little chill all the same. Suddenly, I felt like I hadn't seen him, really seen him, in weeks.

"No!" I agreed. Fourth of July at the beach meant all the sounds: not just the fireworks – and I am talking civilian, purchased down the street with hundreds or thousands of dollars, barely legal fireworks. We got a professional-level show every year just by walking less than a mile to our own beach access and plopping on the sand. The mixture of vacationers without a care in the world and locals showing off provided the best "amateur" shows around. And they went on all… night… long. There were also golf cart parades, which meant the incessant beeping of those pesky recreational vehicles going in reverse for whatever dang reason. There were traffic backups and grocery store madness. It was a different kind of quintessential, and I would miss it a little. I missed the whole family being together, but the version I missed didn't exist anymore. I was determined to focus on the positive this time around.

"We have to make sure there are jars here!"

Paul sat up, much to my regret, and looked at me in fresh bewilderment.

"There are three working toilets, Jess."

"Shush!" I laughed. "I bet there are going to be fireflies! I wonder if the kids have already discovered them."

He sighed softly and put his hand on my back. "I hope so. They haven't been here very long, so maybe they'll discover them with you."

I relished the warmth and especially the reassurance of

his touch. The kids had discovered a lot of things with me in their short, little lives… from the joys of a taco al pastor to baking a perfect cake roll to the nuances of Pearl Jam in the studio versus Pearl Jam live. We watched premieres of Disney movies together – and holiday favorites like *Christmas with the Kranks, How the Grinch Stole Christmas,* and *Eloise at Christmastime.* We read Junie B. Jones books out loud together, cracking up every time she lost her temper and got in trouble. We took golf cart rides to Painter's for ice cream and Benjamin's for donut holes. I went to all of Summer's dance recitals and Jacob's t-ball and soccer games, and I couldn't even get started on Travis, who I'd helped raise for the first few years of his life while Sam and Abby finished college.

And Sam… Sam had been with me since I was nineteen years old, the last mainstay from my life *before* Randall, before the beach, before I grew up and into the person I now was. His siblings made fun of how close we still were, how we talked on the phone every day, but there was a bond between us that I could never explain. Sam had thrown my life into its first real tailspin, and we had navigated it and every subsequent one at least a little bit together.

I was a little afraid his moving away would hurt more than David, my baby, leaving, and maybe even as much as Randall dying, and even admitting that to myself felt so absurd and wrong. And yet…

I turned toward Paul, leaning into his touch, and without a word, he pulled me tightly to him. Our entire marriage had been the result of losses and grief. The first year was bookmarked with upheaval and fear. I wanted our new normal to be a new chapter now, but I sure had my doubts.

"Here. Wear this to the airport."

Katy reached across the little kitchen table and handed Brittney her power accessory, a simple leather cuff bracelet that her mama had bought for her on some random trip to Savannah, or maybe Hilton Head. Mama had not loved her penchant for leather accessories, or black accessories, or red accessories. Those were Katy's trademarks, her musician look. For the last years of Mama's life, she'd been doing more teaching ten-year-olds a few simple guitar chords than she had done gigging, because she had to pay the rent and eighty bucks once or twice a week didn't cut it. Anyway, Mama didn't understand why she wanted to dress the part all the time. "You're not Avril Lavigne. You can wear some wedges or white gold once in a while." Katy would just laugh it off. She wasn't ever going to dress like Mama; that's what she had Danielle, the oldest sister, for.

Julie used to play the part a little, too, but not these days. She'd traded in her designer scrubs for a wardrobe of compression shorts and singlets, because she was always either running or managing the running store she now owned with her husband.

Mama would shake her head, at best. Freak out at worst. At least Danielle still wore Lilly Pulitzer to church on Sundays.

"I can't borrow this," Brittney said. "And I don't need it. I don't think it's going to impress these kids."

Katy shrugged, affixing the cuff back on her own wrist, not sure what else she had to offer. "What does impress adolescent boys, anyway? PlayStation Five? Unlimited Monsters? Christian is only 6 and I've already run out of things to say to him."

"Boys I can handle," Brittney said. She'd grown up with two brothers and an only slightly younger nephew. Katy had lived in a staunchly *girl* house. "The son of a man I am dating is brand new territory. The *bitter* son of that man will be completely alien."

"Hmm…" Katy thoughtfully sipped from her giant tumbler of water, attempting to stay hydrated before the concert that night. She'd been playing bass in El's band for just a few weeks, actually trading off with Harrison – the single dad Brittany was dating – at their shows. Harrison was also El's brother, they were all quasi-roommates, Katy and El were sleeping together, and Harrison was about to move away to be closer to those kids.

Some would call it a circle. Others would call it a circus. But this time last year, Katy's twin sister was preparing to move to Arizona with their younger, not-yet stepbrother. So at least the current situation wasn't the weirdest one.

That's not saying a whoooole heckuva lot. Her mama's voice in her head was usually right on time. It was also sassy as all get out.

And you always pretended to wonder where I got it from, Katy sent back.

She knew her sisters' internal monologues starred Mama, too. But she never asked them if they answered her back. She was too afraid to know the answer, and she didn't need any other reasons to get pegged as the crazy one in the family.

"I'm kinda happy to share this with you," she told Brittney. Brittney nodded absentmindedly while scrolling on her phone. She probably thought Katy meant the brothers, the band, the beach house, the bizarro life situation in general. But she really meant being the black sheep of the family. Brittney really wasn't one, but she felt like she was, so for Katy's purposes, it was almost the same.

"Oh, my God!"

"What now?" They were always distracted with their phones when they were together, but it was on Katy's nerves today. She really needed a non-digital distraction. She was playing the whole show without Harrison there tonight, so he'd be free to entertain his visiting kids, and she was extra twitchy.

"They're not coming!"

Brittney jumped from her chair and was about to bolt… somewhere. "Hold on!" Katy grabbed her wrist. "What? Who?"

"Dakota and Ruthie. They're not coming! Denise

changed her mind about letting them on the plane without her."

"What? They're practically grown. What is her problem?"

"She's a selfish bitch? I don't know. I need to call Harrison."

"Where is he?"

"At the fireworks store probably spending half his paycheck!" She finished the sentence as she was slamming out the door, presumably to call Harrison from the porch.

Well, that was an interesting turn of events. The *plan* had been for Harrison's kids to get to know their Uncle El over the holiday… and get eased into knowing Brittney, too. Harrison had reserved a condo on the ocean, which had likely cost him well over a thousand dollars and was absolutely not refundable.

Not sure what she could do to help, Katy texted Julie about the cancellation, and got the response she should have expected:

WHAT DOES THAT HAVE TO DO WITH YOU?

She was so sanctimonious sometimes.

YOU'RE RIGHT. NOTHING. EXCEPT NOW B & H WILL BE MOPING AROUND HERE THE WHOLE WEEKEND. I WAS LOOKING FORWARD TO SOME FUN TIME WITH EL. ALONE.

THIS IS TRAGIC. I'M TOTALLY HERE FOR YOU, K.

She typed "OH, SHUT UP" and then some other words, and then she just erased it all. Mama would call that the Holy Ghost. She just called it not wanting to deal with Julie's crap.

Her hands still itching and twitching to bounce something off of someone, she started to text El instead. Maybe he would want to have Harrison play that night instead of her.

"So guess what?"

That was Brittney, back again.

"Hmmm?"

"Harrison wants to go see the kids in Virginia instead, and he invited me to go, too."

"What? That's crazy. He's gonna drive in the holiday madness?"

"Well." Brittney grabbed two cans of Bubly from the fridge and passed one to her. "At least we'll be going in the right direction."

"Ha!" Katy wasn't sure if Brittney heard it the same way she did. "That will make for a nice change."

Brittney finished a long swallow before slamming the can back on the table. "What is that supposed to mean?"

Oops. Maybe she did notice.

"Geez. Calm down. I'm just curious. When are you leaving? I thought you had to work this weekend. And what is he going to do about the condo? And… he'll be moving there in a week, right? So…"

Brittney peered at her from squinted eyes. This was a sure sign that Katy was making sense, and no one ever seemed to be okay with that. They were fine with her as long as she was zany and spicy and a little bit dumb. When she sounded smart *and* she disagreed with literally anything, well, that didn't suit their narrative of the stupid baby of the family.

"I didn't ask him, Katy. He wants to see his kids. He asked me to come so I could still meet them. I didn't think I should drill him about the details."

"But Brit, that is what we said we were gonna stop doing… being spontaneous at the cost of being smart. You're going to miss *such* good money if you don't work at Fishwalk this weekend. And that condo—"

"Why do you care so much about our money situation? You've had a real job for like *five minutes*."

"Whoa!" She was right, but *whoa*. "I'm not trying to make it my business. I'm just *saying*."

"Well, don't. He didn't offer any of those details, so I'm not asking. I just need to try to get my shifts covered."

Katy shook her head, no longer caring if she made Brittney mad. She was new to bartending. There wasn't going to be anyone to swap with her. They would all either be on the schedule already or the hell out of this town for the high holiday of summer.

"I'll leave you to it. I have to start getting ready for tonight." It was noon, and the show was at eight, but Katy didn't know what else to say to a sister who was making dumber choices than she was used to making herself.

"I don't think I'd mind working at the Chamber if I got the perks you do," Katy said. She was sitting across from El on the very crowded patio of Neal and Pam's, just a few blocks from his house. Their table was covered with her cheeseburger salad, his Mahi Mahi basket, and two Crooked Hammock Lite lagers between them. Every time she took a breath, she smelled the saltwater air. They had a view of the pier right onto the beach. Tim from Wahoo Creek was playing Jimmy Buffet tunes, and the whole sun-soaked street seemed to be pulsating.

El dragged a tater tot through his tartar sauce (Katy stopped herself from gagging at this as they were still in the polite beginnings of their relationship) and shrugged. "I've worked there a long time. I kinda justify the Friday afternoons off by getting there early almost every day. I couldn't get anything done if I wasn't there before everyone else gets in. They never stop talking. Ever."

"Yeah, but the Fourth? Isn't that a big deal for Myrtle?"

He shrugged again. It almost made Katy self-conscious. She wasn't much of a shrugger. She had strong feelings about everything. "There's a lot going on, but most of it is put on by private businesses. It's a busier weekend for the cops and parks and rec than it is for the Chamber. We got all our madness over with a week or so ago."

"Hmm." Katy thoughtfully chewed a bite, wishing she'd just ordered the black and blue burger instead of trying to trick El into thinking she was a little dainty and trick herself into thinking she was eating healthier. Truth was, she had her mama's metabolism but not her affinity for cardio, so she ate like a toddler some days – peanut butter sandwiches and goldfish crackers, all fairly cheap and filling enough – and like a stoned frat boy other days, preferring wings, fries, those frozen sausage biscuits, coffee with real milk and sugar, and beer. While Julie was running and Danielle was doing 30 days of wall Pilates, Katy never touched a protein shake and rarely exercised beyond some beach bocce ball (beach volleyball was more popular in the movies than it was in Surfside Beach) and heaving around instruments and speakers, be it with the band or at her job at Rogneby's Music School. She looked at El, hoping he saw how strong and lean she was and how *kind of* nonchalant she was trying to be.

"Do you like your job?" she asked. She would soon be starting a new side gig for the Chamber of Commerce, but it was music-based and didn't involve sitting behind a desk. Anything akin to a "little marketing job," which is how El first described his role as Director of Marketing for the Chamber, sounded perfectly horrifying to her.

He smiled at her from behind his glass. "Would it surprise you that I do?"

Her turn to shrug. "Just a little. It seems so different from… how you are on stage, or… who you seem like to me. Director of Anything sounds like someone very serious and important."

El sputtered his beer, and she immediately reddened.

"You know what I mean," she offered feebly.

"It's okay," he cracked. "I never want to come off as serious or overestimate my importance." Her cheeks were absolutely on fire. She wasn't used to guys making her feel shy. "But I do like my job," he continued. "I meet a ton of people and mostly, I am finding out what they do and promoting all the positive things about life here. It's what inspired me to start the band in the first place. You know, Ringo works for the Chamber, too."

"Ringo?" Incredulously, Katy pictured El's dreadlocked, dark-skinned, nonchalant drummer, whose age defied guessing and who seemed to keep a rhythm in his head all the time, saying few words, barely changing his facial expressions, rarely making eye contact. "What does he do?"

"Business development."

Katy mulled that for a second, taking a bite of everything but lettuce. "I don't buy it."

El sputtered. "What? Why?"

"What does he develop? He's a grouch. And a mute. Not that that isn't a whole mood that I entirely respect and even envy, but don't you have to talk to people to develop their businesses?"

El employed Ringo's signature move: he shrugged, again. "We all have different aspects of our personalities, Kakes."

It was hard not to get distracted by his nickname for her. Sweet-as-cake. Kakes. She was not the kind of woman that typically elicited such monikers. She was usually either one of the guys or the girl they just wanted to get in bed. El's view of her was gloriously different.

"Of course, we do," she said. "I'm just really intrigued that a sullen black man with hair like his is a face for the Visit Myrtle Beach website. It's very progressive. And I am amazed he pulls it off. And I am shocked you or Brittney or someone never mentioned it."

"You see how it is, don't you? When we're with the band, it's all band stuff. I barely see him at work, so I don't think about it much. You should ask him about it sometime."

"No way," Katy said, looking longingly at El's tater tots. "He scares me."

El shoved the basket her way and smiled in the way that had been an industrial-strength magnet to her just weeks ago. "Oh, come on, now, Kakes. I don't believe *anything* scares you."

She smiled, dipping a tot not in tartar but ketchup, the proper condiment. It was cold by then and not nearly as good as she wanted it to be. Story of her life, really.

"You'd be surprised," she said, hoping she sounded mysterious and wishing that how he saw her was how she really was.

Jessie

"Abs! It's perfect!"

We had spent approximately seventeen seconds at the magical cabin before our schedule needed to begin. Jacob, who had barely made it to the bank of the creek, had a complete hissy fit over leaving. Paul, who was also wishing we were staying right there for the full three days, probably eating peanut butter out of the jar and holding vigil with the huge porch, firepit, and grill, consoled him with promises of bait-shopping and fishing the next morning… *late* morning.

I sort of didn't want to leave, either, but our trip had a purpose and a timeline. So Abby, Summer, and I climbed into their SUV (she was so excited to be over the mini-van days), while Sam and Jacob joined Paul in the Jeep, and we headed eight miles back through the winding roads to the downtown square of Blairsville, Georgia.

While the guys were solidifying some business at the bank and most likely, the ice cream shop, Abby and I had one thing on our agenda: the tea room. We had owned one ourselves for a moment in time. Named after Abby's late mom, Whitney's came to us at just the right time, we thought. Abby was reeling from grief and burnout. I was fresh from my mercifully short battle with uterine cancer and figuring out what life was supposed to look like *after* everything changes.

The mother of Abby's longtime friend owned her own tea room right here in the cutest little mountain downtown I could have imagined. *Teagan's Room* was so apropos that I giggled as I walked in. There was Irish lace adorning the windows and tables. Bing Crosby was playing from a stereo – yes, a *stereo*, one of those three-piece glorified boom boxes that were all the rage back when I was disappointing my parents and not asking for one for my dorm room because I wasn't going away to college. It sat on top of a hutch adorned by a shamrock tea set. Everything in the room looked straight outta the 1970s. All the chairs were teakwood, all the tables were teakwood except for a few larger ones that were chrome and Formica. And out of the kitchen came a slender woman standing around 5'8, so definitely taller than me, with short gray hair in a relaxed but definite perm, wearing denim slacks – not jeans, but trousers, elastic waistband and all, a flowered blouse, and a contrasting flowered apron. As soon as she opened her mouth, I fell in love with her. My grandmother had an Irish brogue, and the sound of it was like a lullaby to my ears.

"Hello!" She called, casting a distracted smile in our direction, her glance lingering on Summer before she continued scurrying across the room. "Sit at any setting for four you'd like, unless there are more of you coming."

"Mama, doesn't she—"

"Shush." Instinctively, Abby clapped a hand over Summer's mouth. "Just hold a second. Mom, would you like to pick the table?"

The room was empty, so I walked to the middle and sat, beckoning my granddaughter to sit next to me before her mouth got her in trouble. She managed to accomplish both tasks at the same time.

"But I don't understand. I thought you were such good friends. Is this the same tea room you said we would visit and never did?"

Bless her whole heart. I had raised two eleven-year-old girls, right in a row, and the three of us had barely made it out alive. Summer always noticed everything and had reached the tender age when she felt brave enough to say it but was not yet wise enough to read the room.

"Abigail Oakley!" The lilting Irish voice had yelled at full throttle and crossed the floor in just a few long strides. Before Abby could utter a less-patient shush to Summer, they were both wrapped up, those thin arms acting like a vice grip around them. I waited with no ado, gratefully.

"Fiona!" Abby's voice was muffled from inside the embrace. "I wanted to give you a moment before we bombarded you."

"Don't you be silly!" Fiona held Abby at arm's length and studied her face, forgetting about Summer for a moment. "Nessy said you were coming, but I had my days mixed up. We are so thrilled. I didn't know the move was happening so soon."

"Well, we're here for a few days to solidify our plans,

and then we'll be back in a few weeks. We need to get Sam and the kids settled before the school year starts."

Summer looked at her shoes, absolutely hideous yellow Crocs with charms in the shape of suns, sunglasses, and watermelons. They personified her name and were perfect for her age, so I looked at them, too, instead of at her sad face. My parents had stayed in one place their whole lives, so I couldn't imagine moving away from home on the cusp of middle school.

She's resilient. She'll be fine as wine. My late husband's voice often chimed in at just the right time, to either re-assure me or poke fun at my tendency to overthink, and usually, it was both.

"And this must be Jessica?"

I stood, my best practiced smile across my face. I wanted to love Fiona, whom Abby had known since her summer camp days up in Wisconsin, in another life. She would be my girl's lifeline here, and probably a surrogate grandma to Summer and Jacob. I wanted them to have that; but I wanted them with me even more.

"Jessie," I said, offering my hand and my big, fake smile to Summer's new Grandmama. I contemplated how much it would be to rent our precious cabin by the month.

Then I thought of baby Josie at home, and also of Travis – Abby and Sam's oldest who was staying in Myrtle Beach to keep attending Coastal Carolina University and dating his girlfriend. I should be used to my heart being split in half.

Anyway. "It's so nice to meet you. I have heard so much about you…"

"Call me Fi," she said. "And please, make yourselves comfortable. There likely won't be another soul seated in here today before we close, so Summer, love, come and get some menus, and you all stay as long as you like. I'd love to join you if that would be pleasing."

Abby had talked about Fiona and more so, her daughter Vanessa, for as long as I'd known her. "Van," who apparently was also known as "Nessy," had been a counselor at Abby's camp and they'd become friends and remained that way. I'd met Van years ago when she and her young kids came to stay with Abby after the tragic death of her husband, and I had thought of her multiple times since the tragic death of my own husband. My major character trait had always been looking for ways to relate to people, but widowhood was a commonality I could have lived without. I wondered if I would get to know Van now that she and Abby would be practically neighbors.

"Of course we want you to join us," Abby said. She gave Summer a small, forgiving smile and me a small, hopeful smile. She didn't need my permission to invite whomever she wanted to sit at our table. It was a family rule. Hell's bells, it was my life philosophy. But I appreciated that she was protective of my feelings, that she *knew* how I was feeling, even if I was feeling a little bit selfish.

I looked over the tea menu so we could make quick decisions. I wasn't sure how the menfolk would occupy themselves for the hour or so that we were sure to be here, but I tried to relax and not make it my problem. Surely Paul and Sam could figure out how to entertain one child and themselves while we ate a few scones.

I asked Abby to choose my tea as I was feeling indecisive, so she ordered one large pot of spiced raspberry for us to share. Fiona brought it with lemon and honey, along with a tiered platter of blueberry scones, veggie cream cheese tartlets, and mini quiche Lorraine. Everything looked simple and beautiful, and for a moment, I missed my tea room so much I wanted to call Maggie and tell her I changed my mind.

Shut up Jessie. It isn't like you can't just go there whenever you want to eat or cook or serve or run the place.

For once, the voice in my head did not belong to either of my husbands or to Maggie, but to me. In the midst of everything seemingly changing all the time, I had to learn to trust myself.

We tucked in to all of Fiona's delicious offerings. I was halfway through my second scone (not what I needed, but those fresh berries were irresistible) when another woman walked in. There was no hesitation or formality about it. All 4'11 of Van, in her signature untied Chuck Taylors, an overloaded messenger bag at her hip, and a harried look on her face, marched across the room and dove straight into Abby's arms, practically sitting in her lap. Summer looked at them slack jawed. She hadn't seen Van since she was practically a baby, and Abby wasn't typically one to be wrapped up so easily. They were certainly a sight.

The embrace lasted; Summer looked awkward, Fiona got up to get some sort of refill, no doubt, while I just ate my scone. I was used to sisterly affection—I was blessed to share it with Maggie and to witness it with my own girls. Abby was part of that; she'd been in our family since she was nineteen years old. But she was also outside of it. She was one of two children, and her mother was gone. Her father lived a mere ninety minutes from this quaint little town, but he wasn't here greeting and helping his daughter. Fiona and Van were. She had known Van even longer than she knew us, and I exhaled with a little relief that she'd still have a sister nearby in this big life change she was making.

"Nessy, sit down, for Christ's sake!" Fiona sounded stern, but her lips were turned upward in a smile. She set a sweating cold bottle of Dr. Pepper in front of her daughter's still vacant seat, and I smiled knowingly. When I owned my tea room for a fleeting moment, half my family wanted to drink anything but the tea.

Van (Nessy? Who could keep track?) removed herself from Abby, kissed her mama's cheek, threw her bag on the floor with a thud, and slumped into her seat. She took a long drink and then widened her big hazel eyes as they landed on me.

"Mama Jessie! I didn't even see you there! You look… I mean… wow!"

Summer sighed loudly upon being ignored again. I almost giggled, because I was just as vain as any adolescent girl and enjoyed being noticed for my appearance from time to time. I had probably lost thirty pounds of body weight and two tons of stress since I had last seen Van, so though a good decade and a half had passed, I looked a good bit livelier. She bounded back up from her seat, and thankfully hugged Summer and kissed the top of her head before she embraced me, and I kissed the top of *her* head.

We really didn't have friends. We made family.

Fiona's face still showed a contrast between warm amusement and the edge of impatience. She had resumed her seat and lifted her cup, which she had brought from the kitchen. I watched her sip, close her eyes, and lean back in her chair. She was the queen of her castle. I loved it.

Summer was yapping away, happy to finally bask in the attention of a new audience. Van started telling her about the local dance studio, where her daughter took classes, and Fiona rushed back to the kitchen to fetch some lavender honey as soon as Summer said she'd always wanted to try it. Abby flushed in irritation at that, and I understood, but I also just shrugged at her. Summer was going through a lot, too. Let them spoil her a little.

"Do they have lyrical there, because I was finally old enough to take it at home, and—"

"Evie takes lyrical!" Fiona answered, scooting right back in with a gorgeous miniature porcelain pitcher, painted with dragonflies and filled with honey for her little highness. "Well, she did…"

"Mama!" Van's eyes darkened and her tone shifted into a sharp one. "Later. Please." Then she smiled toward Summer and Abby. "They have everything there. Registration won't be long after you move here, so you'll be just in time." She winked at Summer, and I wondered what was up with her own daughter, whom I knew to be in her early teen years.

Summer engaged endlessly after that. Van and Abby sent messages through their eyeballs and, I noted, via text a few times. Fiona side-eyed her daughter in between fussing over the rest of us. I mostly just sat there and sipped tea. I could have eaten a dozen more scones, but other than politely asking Fiona about her recipe, I was as silent and useless as one of the empty platters. I was watching Summer's mouth form words but had no idea what she was talking about, wondering if Paul would lose patience and come whisk us, or at least, me, back to the whimsical cabin soon.

The door did fly open just then, but instead of my husband sauntering through, a long-legged teen girl rushed inside. Her black leotard was covered with a crotched and somewhat ratty grey sweater. She wore classic pink tights with holes running up and down the legs and equally classic black and white checkerboard Vans on her feet. Her brown hair was arranged in two elaborate braids and twisted into a bun, and her face, half-covered with large, cat-eye sunglasses with emerald green frames, was twisted into a scowl. She was headed straight for Van.

"Mother. Really? You told Ms. Shay I was *grounded* from my *class*? My *pointe* class? Isn't that, if nothing else, a colossal waste of money? It's summer! What else am I supposed—"

"Evie, shut your gob!" Fiona hissed, jumping up and standing at her side, giving Van a glower that rivaled her granddaughter's. "Why don't you go to the kitchen and get a sandwich from the cooler?"

"Because I'm not hungry, Grandma!"

"¡Ni pensarlo!" Van snapped, every bit her Puerto Rican father's daughter, I imagined. "Mamá, you will not let her speak to you that way! Evie, in the kitchen."

The two of them stomped off practically in unison. Fiona, cut from a much different cloth than I, followed them.

Any one of my kids would have shot poison darts from their eyeballs straight through me if I meddled in a moment like that. I contemplated reaching for a completely excessive third pastry, but opted instead to say, "Abs. You think we should go?"

She rolled her eyes. "Sam has texted me six times in

the last two minutes, so, yeah. Let me just… Ugh."

I waited her out.

"Evie was caught in some… trouble… last week," Abby said, casting her eyes toward Summer, like I couldn't tell from the tone of her voice and the entire exchange that something was wrong that a younger child didn't need to hear. She turned toward the kitchen door. "I don't want to leave without saying goodbye."

"Go knock on the door. I'll leave money."

"She's not going to let us pay."

"We'll wait outside," I called, leaving a fifty-dollar bill on the table and taking Summer by the hand. I had enough family drama of my own.

We almost made it to the door when Evie came crashing out of the kitchen. A flood of tears coursed down her cherubic face, her black mascara making angry tracks on her pink cheeks. She ran right to Abby, who gave her the necessary Mama Hug and looked at me to help decipher what Evie was saying –

"They… don't… understand… ANYTHING!" *Oh, boy.* Her gaping sobs muddied the words, but I had more than enough context to interpret. "Just because… he's…he's… older and… goes to a different school. They won't…. They won't… Mami won't let me see him!"

Danger, danger! I almost laughed at Paul's voice in my head. He had sworn he was all used up when it came to teenage girls. Any future granddaughter drama would be mine to handle. And here I was, and she wasn't even mine.

I braced myself as Abby asked some questions, and Evie managed to summarize her woes: There was a boy dancer at the studio. He was about to be a senior. So what if Evie was only a freshman? Evie's family didn't know him (and/or probably didn't like him). She had lied to stay after classes and spend time with him, so she was being threatened with having to quit dance or be supervised by her grandfather. Absolute, teenage-girl horror.

Abby said all the good things to say. "Give it time. Your mama just loves you. She wants to protect you." *Blah blah blah* is all Evie would hear. She dried her eyes and flashed a wan smile at Abby, exiting to wait for Van outside.

Abby looked at me, suddenly not caring that Summer could hear. "He's almost eighteen. She wants to be able to 'hang out' at his house, and since Van won't let her, she's gone all tortured-poet-teenager. No one wants her to be happy or have love in her life." She shrugged. I bet she wouldn't shrug if we were talking about Summer. God bless.

"Well," I said, one former-pregnant-teen-mother to another. "There's only one way to keep brave and stupid teenagers from their chosen destructive destinies."

"Yeah?" Abby said, a knowing tone in her voice. "What's that?"

I looked pointedly at Summer. "Pray."

AT LEAST I AM NOT THE ONLY INDECISIVE AIRHEAD IN THE FAMILY ANYMORE.

She should have felt bad, but Katy was relieved on more than one level when Brittney sent her a flurry of text messages detailing more changing plans. She and Harrison had remembered they possessed the good sense God gave a goat and decided to stay in town, at the rented condo on the beach. Brittney was still going to work her shifts and enjoy the festivities (she could sleep when she was dead), and she would meet the kids eventually, and Harrison would maybe calm down enough to enjoy their last weekend together before his move.

So they would all be at The Fishwalk that night – that is, Ed's Fishwalk Tavern, which was one of El's favorite places for The Salty Lips to play and where Brittney had been working as a bartender for approximately fifteen minutes. Katy would be playing bass, El would be singing and running the show, Brittney would be slinging drinks to excited tourists and impatient locals who should know better, and Harrison would likely be brooding somewhere in the midst of that. Maybe they should get him to play a few songs.

She pivoted in the full-length mirror, the one that Brittney had thankfully convinced El to hang. Honestly, El was just prissy enough that he seemed to use it as much as Katy did. She smiled, thinking of the sight of him, his legs hugged by fitted jeans and his chest by Onno t-shirts, the closest he could wear to satisfy his need to be neat and tidy and still pull off his alt-rock singer persona. He was so different from anyone she had dated before, mature and together and confident without being a boring prat or narcissistic pig. She probably should have set her standards higher long ago.

Her own appearance, well, she used to feel surer of it. She certainly looked like a beach girl with her long blond hair that got lighter at the ends, an easy tan, and fabulous metabolism that lent itself to lean limbs and a taut belly in spite of her propensity to eat like a twelve-year-old set loose in a 7-11. But she hadn't changed her style since she was basically a teenager. There wasn't a lot of style required of a part-time music teacher, part-time gigger. When she lived in Wilmington, she blended in just fine in her beach attire, only she would be sure to ditch her cutoff jeans for full-length ones, sans holes, when she was giving lessons. Now that she was back in Myrtle, well, Surfside, her entire wardrobe was shorts and tanks. When she went to work at Rogneby's Music School, she made sure the shorts were a little longer and the necks were a little higher. When necessary, she added an oversized band tee or maybe a hoodie.

She looked boring. But it was too late to do anything about it before that night. She sat in front of the mirror to work on her makeup, just as Brittney crashed into the bedroom.

"Hey!—" she started, frustrated. And then she remembered that she did the same thing to Brittney all the time.

"I'm about to be late for the shift I almost didn't show up for," she exhaled. "But I just heard El on the phone, and you know, sisters before misters."

Katy rolled her eyes, but she was grateful for the loyalty. El had been Brittney's best friend long before Katy became her stepsister.

"Okay... what?" She narrowed her eyes at her reflection. Maybe since it was July third, she should wear red instead of black. But her bass was red, and the contrast looked cool, so...

"His ex is in town."

Crap. Which one?

"The only one that counts very much... Atalaya."

Ata-flippin-laya. Of course it was her. She was El's most serious ex-girlfriend. They had lived together for years before she broke up with him to move to Savannah, which was probably her middle name, to manage a spa chain, and marry a golf pro named Brody. *Atalaya.* She came from old money, as far as the beach was concerned. Her father owned half the land in the county and from what Brittney had told her, always looked down on El, whose mother was unstable at best and not one you want in the *Grand Strand* magazine wedding feature.

Katy steeled herself against her increasing heart rate. She didn't want to care about this. She turned back to the mirror and lined her upper eyelids a bit more, going for the smokey effect even though it was much more dramatic than her usual nude with a little glitter look. She added slate-colored eye shadow, and then her best mascara, the kind she saved for special occasions, with little fibers that cost way too much, and then her "angel dust" golden-flecked glitter. It was silly. No one would be close enough to see her face, except for the band, and they'd all be busy playing.

Brittney cleared her throat. Katy had forgotten she was there.

"So, um," she started, embarrassed. "How did you come by this information?"

"My old friend Madison from the Chamber. Atalaya worked there, too, for like, a minute, before she went to one of the ad agencies. Tourism wages were not what she signed up for."

"I'm sure." Katy raised her eyebrows in appraisal, finally satisfied. Then she turned to Brittney at last. "What else did Madison from the Chamber have to say?"

"Mmm. Well, her husband is with the PGA in Michigan and that didn't suit her holiday needs, so she's visiting her old beach haunts with friends this weekend…"

"And…?"

"Why do you think I know more than that?"

"Because you do!" Katy said, swatting her arm. "What? Did you internet stalk her or did Madison from the Chamber have more details?"

"She's Madison the Sadistic PT now," Brittney mocked. "Sam went to her for his knee and—"

"I don't care about Madison!" Katy snapped. "Can you just tell me what you want to tell me? Am I this annoying?"

She already knew the answer to that and had a sneaking suspicion she knew what else Brittney was going to say.

"Madison mentioned that they'll be hanging at the Fishwalk tonight…"

"Of *course* they will. Is it because of El, or are we all pretending it's not?"

"The latter," Brittney sighed, sitting on the bed. "I mean, when Atalaya worked at the Chamber, Ringo was her boss…"

What the what? Katy was starting to feel like she was in bizarro world with all the circular connections, apparently the result of her peer group being professional while she was being a gypsy. "Is Ringo his real name? Like his government name? Like, I can't even picture him having employees or sitting behind a desk or wearing a shirt with sleeves."

Brittney shrugged. "It's the name on his bio on the Chamber website. That's all I know."

"Whatever. And that's all you know about Ata-flippin-laya? She and her entourage are showing up?"

"Yep." Brittney scooted off the bed and sat on the floor next to her. "They are everything obnoxious. But El couldn't care less what she does anymore. I just wanted you to know… because *I'm* your entourage."

Katy turned and raised her eyebrows, not wanting her to see how intimidated she was by the idea of a Beach Belle named after a local castle, not wanting to care so much about what El would think when he saw her, not knowing what to say by this show of loyalty by someone who wasn't her biological sister.

"And your smoky eyes are *totally* on point," Brittney

continued. "You need setting spray?"

There. It appeared they were in this, whatever it was going to be, together.

The first set was fine. Katy's nerves caused a small timing issue in the first transition, but by "Give It Away," she found the pocket, exhaled a little, and flirted with the lead singer... her lead singer. At every show, when Ringo took the lead during the third verse, the crowd always went a little wild, so El seized the opportunity to kiss Katy on the mouth. Shocked – and roused – she almost lost her rhythm again, but when she didn't, a surge of something went through her. She felt powerful. A goddess of rock. And that thought made her laugh really hard for a second and almost lose her place again.

El shook his head, grinning widely at her. *Focus,* she willed herself, right as El reclaimed the lead. They were only just getting started, but dang it if that man didn't set her stomach to roller coasterin'.

They stayed status quo for a few songs, nothing to get riled about. Katy fixed her eyes on Brittney, working behind the bar, right in her eyeshot. She felt a surge of something different – was it pride? – watching her stepsister slide from customer to back bar to cash register, smiling and singing along. Who knew Ms. Marketing Exec would be so much happier living the bohemian weirdo life?

Geno strummed the opening drive of "Run," one of Katy's favorites to hear El sing, and it was right then that something else at the bar caught her eye: a petite, golden princess, void of a crown, but sparkling nonetheless in white shorts trimmed in lace, a white halter, white heeled sandals, and bleached blond extensions flowing in beachy waves down her bare back. She was surrounded by four or five clones, dressed in shades of white with plenty of skin showing and hair that was much more *done* than what most women bothered with on a sticky July night at an outside dive bar. Though her face was not easily distinguished from the stage (*hellfire and damnation if Daddy wasn't right and she actually didn't have perfect vision anymore*), Katy was certain this was Ata-flippin-laya.

Just keep playing. He's yours. The voice in her head was Julie's, and she needed to shake that and everything else off if she was going to keep her place in these songs, which were pretty new to her. Hellfire and damnation to Harrison, too, who had refused to play at all tonight. He was just sitting at the bar looking miserable unless Brittney was talking to him. Katy was equal parts excited to play in a band and scared to death that she had overplayed her hand and was in no way up to this level of performing.

She made her way through ten more songs, including the set finale, "Breath," which involved El seemingly getting deep in his feelings and screaming alt-rock-emo style by then end. It always gave her a little chill to hear it. Maybe some vocalists could fake that, but she was getting to know El pretty well and didn't think *he* could fake that; and she almost didn't want to think about what had happened in his life – tragically losing his other brother, for one – that he tapped into for that sort of emotion.

I will be the death of you. With that, the first set was over, Katy was sweating, a bit spent, and a lot exhilarated. She tried not to keep her eyes fixed on Atalaya, but as El came next to her to plant another kiss, this time on her cheek. He said, "Awesome job" in her ear, and she wasn't sure if she believed him, but before she could ask, he kept walking. She set her bass on its stand, stretched her tired back, and watched him.

He walked directly toward Atalaya.

Katy gave in to her instinct to sit on her amp and stare. She gathered the sweaty tendrils of hair off her neck, holding them up in a makeshift bun, and fanned herself with her other hand. That did nothing to cool her off. She needed water. And she wanted a drink of something else. She had fifteen minutes, but she was stuck.

"You gotta hydrate."

She looked up to see her bandmate Geno at her shoulder, surprised she hadn't smelled him first. Playing in the July humidity was no joke for any of them. She tried not to wrinkle her nose and murmured, "I know. I'm going."

"Who's El talking to? Is that what's her face?"

Katy stood next to the guitarist, his brown curls dripping sweat and the ever-present smell of flour from his day job as a bread baker wafting in the air. Her eyes confirmed where she figured El would stop. Atalaya was looking up at him from under her mile-long fake lashes. El's face was expressionless; he was a professional and needed to use the intermission wisely just like the rest of them.

So why did he go to her? The bathroom is on the other side of the bar.

"I guess it is," Katy answered. "I don't really know."

Geno scoffed. "Yeah, you do." He gave her a playful punch on the shoulder. "Go. He has to talk to everyone. He doesn't kiss everyone in the middle of a song."

Since she wasn't known for being mysterious, Geno knowing exactly what she was watching and thinking wasn't much of a surprise.

"'K!" she answered, faking breeziness. "You need anything from the bar?"

"I'm all set," he answered, so she had no choice but to jump off the stage and head to the bar, by way of El. Nothing else would make sense.

He was already walking away from Atalaya, toward the restrooms, but Katy couldn't change her trajectory without being obvious. *Why? Why do I care?* She brushed briskly past the entourage, barely a step away when she heard, "Well, he had no place to go but down."

She knew better, but she turned on her heel and confirmed what she thought: one of Atalaya's crones was staring her up and down, a few of the others were smirking, and Atalaya herself looked not admonished but haughty.

"Hope you girls are enjoying the show." It was weak, but all she could think of that wouldn't betray her anger or worse, her curiosity.

"It's a show alright." The clone who spoke sported mermaid highlights, ample breasts spilling out of her halter, and shorts that played peek-a-book with the kind of glutes rappers wrote songs about. "Trailer trash picking up Atalaya's discards. I guess it fits."

Katy turned around. She shouldn't have. She *knew* that. But "trash" was one word she wouldn't abide. She got that from her daddy.

She stared Mermaid Hair up and down. Didn't change her facial expression. Didn't think of her older sister Danielle who had struggled with body image since puberty. She just spoke in a monotone voice and said, "At least something fits around here." Then she turned on her heel and walked away.

The outraged reactions followed her. "Aw, naw" and

"Come say that again, *ma'am*" and of course the inevitable, "Little bitch." It didn't matter who had said what, and she wouldn't turn around for a million dollars. *Please Katy. You would turn around for ten dollars or a Mic Ultra,* Julie's voice reminded her. She strolled toward the bathroom, though she wanted to storm, and counted down from thirty while she did her business and maneuvered her sweaty shorts back in place. Crap, one of them had probably been Brittney's old pal Madison. She had to tell her, but Brit would be way too busy behind the bar.

Katy would have to be a big girl and a lone ranger.

And she would absolutely need a shot.

Anyway, she was reminded as she stepped out, she was not alone. She had a band. Heck, she had a band of brothers. She didn't see El, but Ringo and Geno and their keyboard player Mikey were standing right there, with a tequila and a lime waiting for her. El had them on a strict one-shot-per-set limit. Otherwise, they jumped over the fine line from good and loose to unfocused and shit-for-brains before the second set was half over.

"Here's to Katy Bug's first official night!" Mikey said. They drained their glasses.

"Is it?" Geno asked.

"Without her six-foot-two, hairy training wheels," Ringo muttered. She could barely hear him over the background noise and was barely paying attention as she tried to scan for her new arch-nemeses, but that made her sputter. She'd been so distracted by Friggen Atalaya, she'd forgotten all about Harrison. Why wasn't he playing some, anyway?

Katy glanced over at Brittney, who was still bustling. One of her customers was dressed in a white sundress with her hair in a messy braid around her shoulder and holding a hot pink, sparkly cell phone case that was catching all the light. Had she been one of the royal court?

She turned her head in Katy's direction and glared, first at her, then back at Brittney. *Hm. Yep.*

Brittney rolled her eyes and shrugged. Katy *thought* for sure she was probably defending her, saying Katy was in the zone for the show and didn't want to mess with anybody. But Katy also felt her face get hot and the hamster wheel start turning uncontrollably in her head. What if? What if Brittney was rolling her eyes *at* her? *About* her?

What if you remembered that you're a grown ass adult and the people who love you, love *you?*

That was Mama. Mama's voice could not be ignored. Katy smiled at her band bros and took a gulp of water from the cup that had materialized where her empty shot glass had been. El had also materialized right behind her, and he was beaming at her.

"Do not feed the animals," he said. His hands went to her hips. "This is your night."

"It's kinda hard—"

"Nope." He moved one hand over her mouth. She couldn't help it. She licked it. They both laughed. And then Brittney was in front of them.

"Almost time," Ringo said, and he punched Katy's shoulder, then El's as he walked away. Geno and Mikey followed, lost in their own barbs and their own world.

"So that's Madison," Brittney said with a smirk. She pushed Katy's water toward her. "Drink the rest of this." She obeyed. And then Brittney shoved another shot glass at her. "Don't worry, El. It's half lemonade."

Katy downed it without a word.

"I'm just topping her off. They're probably going to start something," Brittney continued, "So she might need it."

"No one is starting anything, and Katy is fine." El's eyes started to blaze angrily. Inwardly, Katy did a duck and cover. She should never have…

"Kakes? Don't worry about them. Or this. Brit? Don't feed the animals. You know better."

He stormed off; well, he didn't quite storm. His legs were long, and so was his stride, and he looked in a hurry even when he wasn't. Katy watched him get his ear monitors back in place and pick up his mic. She stood.

"I gotta go. Do you really think…?"

Brittney shook her head. "I gotta go, too, but… I'll tell Ed to keep an eye on them. He doesn't wany any shenanigans. The crowd is probably about to pick up."

That made Katy's tummy lurch. She sort of regretted the second half-shot.

"Okay. Thanks, sis." She hurried back up to the stage. Dave, the other guitar player and the elder statesmen of The Salty Lips, looked sideways at her. "We gonna have a cat fight?"

Dave always had a cup of orange… something… in his microphone stand. He swore it was Mio drops. She wondered if it wasn't something more… magical. He played like fire and seemed like he never broke a sweat over anything.

She grinned at him. "Let's hope not."

He grinned, quite widely, back. "Let's hope *so*."

Laughing, they started the next song. Katy watched the white walkers sway back and forth to the "The Middle," holding their hard seltzers and alternating smirks and scowls toward the stage. She wondered if maybe the century old, huge-and-majestic oak tree that shaded half of the outdoor dining area would fall over on them.

She managed to ignore them, or at least pretend to ignore them. And then it was time for one of her favorite songs to hear and one of the scariest for her to play. She took a deep breath and held it for a moment. All she had to do was kick it off and get through the opening bars with their weird timing, and then it was mellow for a minute. Surely, she could do that.

She placed her fingers where they belonged, and Atalaya's girls — all of them save for the queen herself, flipped the bird in her direction, nice and low, at their waists, so only the ones on stage would see.

Refusing to react, she charged ahead and started "Better Man." The opening went fine. Then she had to wait forever through an entire verse and chorus and half of another verse. The white walkers were singing every word at the top of their lungs, still starting at her. And then, as the whole band came in full throttle, Katy completely lost her timing. Dave shot her a look that clearly said, "Get it together, you dumb kid," while El just raised an eyebrow at her. Oh, bless it, she was going way too fast. She turned around to Ringo and followed his rhythm until she pulled herself back together. Her stomach flipped. She definitely should not have shot tequila or paid any attention to anything off the stage.

All the voices in her head converged, simultaneously telling her it was fine and no big deal and also to put the bass down and go finish the business off stage. When El's voice faded out at the end of the last "better maaaaaaaaaaaaaaaaaan," he turned around to start his sexy, grungy jumps and smiled at her. She looked toward Ringo while smiling back. This was the most fun part of the song to play.

You ain't gonna find a better man. That was her own voice. As the song ended, one voice rang out over the diminishing bars. "Find a better GIRL, El!"

That time, everyone reacted except for her. Dave looked at her, rolled his eyes, shook his head. El's hands scrunched into balls. Mikey muttered something loudly enough for, hopefully, only the band to hear. Geno came up from behind her and just stood at her shoulder, all full of the solidarity. And Ringo, bless him, just started the next song.

"That was the longest set in the history of hot-ass nights," Mikey said. "Who wants a beer?"

A few grunts and nods resounded, and everyone but El and Katy followed him off the stage. Dave was already thronged by a few of his fans; he played in several bands around town and always seemed to have wanna-be groupies in attendance. El turned to Katy and lifted her bass off her shoulder.

"I got it," she said, defensively.

"I know you do," he said. "But I want to help. You did great tonight." He set the bass on its stand and took her hand in his.

"You don't have to say that."

"Kakes, you *did*. Don't let stupid crap take that away from you."

"Stupid crap was losing my place—"

"No one is perfect. Geno lost his place twice. I forgot the Offspring words. Dave almost knocked over his microphone stand…"

She did the only thing she could think of; she shrugged. "Elliot."

A sharp female voice with a full-on southern accent called his name. Katy didn't even have to look. Sure enough, the Queen was standing at the edge of the stage, arms crossed, hands tightly wound around a White Claw and an iPhone Max Pro, tapping her foot like someone owed her something and was late making the payment.

El turned around, but he didn't answer her.

"Are you going to talk to me? And are you going to make this woman apologize?"

El cocked his head to one side. Katy knew the transformation by then, from rocker-boyfriend-bro-kinda guy to Chamber of Commerce Executive and Mouthpiece Guy.

"I did talk to you. And I'm not aware of any apologies that need to be made from Katy, although from what I witnessed, several are due her."

"She *insulted* Taylor. She *body-shamed* her. I mean—"

El held up his other hand. Katy looked at the tattooed words running up his right forearm. *Exodus 14:14.* The reference wasn't there, just the words. "The Lord will fight for you; you need only to be still." She'd thought it was crazy from the get-go that he was branded with the same verse her mama used to repeat to her. She used to always want a fight. She did not want this one. She did not want to lose.

"Does Brody know you're here?"

"Excuuuuuse me? What does that have to do with this, this—"

"Atalaya. If you call her a name, I might let go of her, and my girl is wild. There's no telling what she might do."

Katy couldn't even stifle her snicker. Suddenly, her

boldness returned, just as Atalaya's face morphed into rage.

"Your *girl?* Is she really? Elliot, look how far you've come. You don't have to… I mean… can't we… You don't belong with someone wild, not after I worked so hard to get you tamed."

Oof. What Katy didn't know about El was plenty, but she knew well enough that she squeezed his hand in restraint, and with no hesitation, no internal voice admonishing her, she stepped in front of him.

"You might have known him when you were fresh outta Horry-Georgetown, flaunting your little human resources certificate like it qualified you to run the world. But now that you're one of the real housewives of the turf, you're not even close to in his league. You didn't tame him. You tried to stifle him because he was too much for you. So why don't you take your little wedgy-making jumpsuit and your drunken Botox harpies and go back to the player's club? It's *tame* and stuffy and boring there, and you'll be right at home. El doesn't *want* you here."

The effect was as if she had punched Atalaya in the stomach. The air left her. She looked frantically at El.

"Elliot, is she for real? I just wanted to *talk* to you."

"You just wanted to try and make me miss you."

"Ha." She bucked right back up. "I'm a *married* woman. Happily married."

Katy answered, "Then why are you here telling your very ex-boyfriend about it? Go play with Brody and his balls."

El snorted. He put his arm around Katy's shoulders and gave that signature shrug. "Hon, we really don't have anything to say to each other. I'm sorry the sport wasn't what you were looking for tonight, but we've all moved on. We're just making music and having a beer and going home. Maybe you should head down to the Marshwalk and find some other drunk people at Dead Dog. They'll be more interested in playing with you."

"Okay, *Willie Nelson*." Yet another of the white walkers appeared at Atalaya's elbow, sticking out from her jutted hip. She was still looking at El and Katy incredulously. "You go play your little songs and we will… 'Laya, let's go back to the beach house. This whole thing was lame."

"And *limp*!" she added venomously, narrowing her eyes at El before huffing away.

El kept laughing. Katy relished the feeling of his arm around her, like she won something, but the best part was: there was never a contest. He was for real. They were for real.

"Want a Corona?" he asked.

"Absolutely. Two—"

"Two limes," he finished. The show was over. The night was just starting.

I WOKE UP WITH MY HEAD ON PAUL'S
bare chest. The AC was working overtime on my behalf
and though my fifteen-year battle with hot flashes, made
worse after radiation, was the reason, our bedroom was an
igloo, and I was certain we were covered in frost.

He was nestled with me under the luxurious comforter,
sleeping as one does when there is no light and no ambient
noise and one's wife has driven him insane for the past...
well, two years. After the abrupt ending to our tea party, the girls and I reconnected with our guys in the town
square, drove to three different houses, made a grocery
stop at the Ingles for our Fourth of July provisions, had
the *best* barbecue dinner imaginable at a roadside place
called Jim's Smokin' Que, and then made a bonfire for the
kids, complete with s'mores, while reading through Sam
and Abby's shiny new lease on the first house we saw.

And there were *fireflies*.

Then I stayed up watching three episodes of *Fuller House* with Summer, and *then* we decided to watch our favorite *Gilmore Girls* ("The Festival of Living Art"), and by the time I got Jacob some water and dragged myself to the bed, Paul was deeply unconscious. And I felt guilty; he knew this would happen, that we would get here and all my energy would go into making it an Amazing, Fabulous, Magical Memory for Summer and Jacob, and making things as easy as possible for Sam and Abby, and yes, try to soak it all up for myself, as a salve to my broken heart.

And Paul got the bed to himself for two hours and a wife who was not only sad but also exhausted.

I internal-monologued myself to sleep with: *I will do better in the morning. There is no to-do list for tomorrow. Feed ourselves. Enjoy ourselves. That is* all.

Morning in sight, I brushed my lips against him and listened intently, hearing nothing but the loud whirring of the AC. No sunrise yet. No dog to let out. I felt secure that the kids were still sleeping and willed myself to return to unconsciousness. It was too late, though. The to-do list started ticking in my brain. We had bucked tradition once again and decided to grill pizzas for our Fourth of July cookout. Seemed simple enough, not much prep, but that didn't matter. The internal scrolling was in full swing: *Did we remember to get pepperoni? I wonder if the little grocer at the end of the road has any. Do we have enough s'more fixings and ice cream in case Abby's friends come over for dessert? This town is really small. The stores might not even be open today.* And then, when I had exhausted all those possibilities, thoughts turned to home, where my oldest grandson was house-and-dog-sitting for us. *Is Travis walking Dolly or just letting her out for a quick minute at a time? Is she peeing all over the house? Is he entertaining Cali there? If we catch it on the ring camera, should I tell Sam? Good Lord, Jessie. When did you become such a prudish old lady? I really like this cabin, but I really miss my bed. Is Brit doing okay at The Fishwalk this weekend? I still can't believe she's paying off student loans by being a bartender. Randall would be turning in his grave if we hadn't cremated him. That's morbid, Jess. You'll make Mikayla cry. Mikayla can't hear you. She's been super sensitive the last few weeks, though. Oh, my. She might be pregnant! Nope. Don't even think about it. We just got through Danielle's pregnancy. Okay. Change of subject. I wonder if Maggie is re-opening the tea room tomorrow or taking an extra holiday. Not your problem, Jess. Not. Your. Problem. I wonder if I'll ever get off the waitlist for American Riviera Orchard. I bet the candles at Sunrise Grocery are just as great of quality as whatever Meghan is selling on there.*

"Oh my God. I can *hear* you."

"Oh my God, was I saying all that out *loud*?"

Paul's telltale shaking started. He was laughing at me. What a way to wake up… with an ugly laugh. I shifted my head, smiled into his neck, and waited for him to catch his breath. "You're vibrating," he said.

Ah. Yeah. I did that sometimes. It's why my doctor, Paul, and my kids collectively convinced me to start on a low dose of Prozac.

I really needed to get that refilled.

"There's just a lot going on," I said, immediately regretting it.

He'd stopped laughing. "Jess, remember yesterday? Like less than twenty-four hours ago? We said we'd have some downtime, maybe take a nap? You ran us all ragged last night. What exactly do you have going on today?"

"Nothing. I just mean… everywhere. At home. I don't know." I was already a little embarrassed by my worries, but they would be no surprise to Paul.

"We have enough food to feed everyone back at home," he said, reading my thoughts. "And Abby already told the kids they're not staying with us tonight. And frankly, the ones who are back at home are probably happy to be rid of us for a hot minute. So—"

"I know," I sighed. Even Randall hadn't been able to hear me *think* the way Paul did. "Are you ready for pancakes or do you want to sleep a little longer?"

He sighed, deeply, dramatically. "I *want* to sleep more, but you said 'pancakes' and now that's all I can think about."

I giggled. I had made concessions, so breakfast was a simple plan of pre-cooked bacon and Bisquick pancakes on the grill. And coffee… *all* the coffee.

"I don't believe you," I teased, stroking his leg with my foot. It was still awfully early, and—

"If we cook now, it will get cold before the kids are awake," Paul said, finishing another of my thoughts.

"Guess we better wait then," I said, and I kissed him, suddenly relieved morning hadn't quite broken just yet.

Eight hours and two meals later, I was ready for a nap. I had no regrets about how Paul and I had (as quietly as possible) spent the pre-sunrise moments of the morning, nor about the gathering taking place at our perfect, magical rented cabin. But I had to concede that he was right about so many things, and at the top of the list was his wife's utter exhaustion.

We'd kept our cookout simple with pre-made crusts and everyone choosing their own toppings. At first it was only the six of us, eating on the porch with paper plates in our laps, taking turns at the creek with the two fishing poles we found in a closet, listening to Kenny Chesney on the outdoor speakers, and verbally arranging Sam and Abby's new home. But on the edge of the afternoon, just as a nap in one of those splendid rocking chairs was starting to sound tantalizing and seem possible, a dusty green Ford Explorer pulled into the gravel driveway. We'd extended an invite to Fiona, Van, et al. to eat with us at one o'clock. At that point it was after two, and Van was purposefully marching toward the porch, followed by a sheepish and gangly adolescent boy, trailing behind her looking as though being there was tantamount only to going straight to hell in an already fiery handbasket.

"Sorry," she said, already up the steps and leaning over Abby's chair in the sisterly half-nuzzle. "I finally gave up fighting with Evie. And Himself here didn't want to come either—" Van looked over at me and rolled her eyes, as though I was in on it, which, of course, gave me a delightful sense of inclusion and immediate empathy toward her. "—but feeding a twelve-year-old boy practically requires a third job, so… here we are. I hate being late, but unfortunately, it's who I am at this point in life."

Paul, sitting next to me with a half-gallon sized tumbler of sweet tea, barely seemed to register this information. He was functionally a father of five daughters now, and six if we threw Abby in the mix, so the drama ante needed to be a lot higher in order to faze him. But Sam looked over at me from his chair, a bit stricken. He had hopes that life in the mountains would bring less chaos, and Van definitely symbolized the opposite.

"It's totally fine," Abby said, getting up. She shot Sam a look, and he stood, too. "Let's get you guys some food. Everything's inside."

"I'm not hungry," came a mutter from the bottom of the stairs.

"Just get inside," Van snapped, without looking back. He dutifully followed her, not casting a glance at Paul or Jacob, who weren't paying attention, or at Summer and me. We definitely were.

After what I could only assume was an awkward and quick meal, Abby and Van came back outside with a tray holding little bowls of berries and cream. It had been my other acquiescence to simplicity for the day; no trifles or shortcakes or "homemade damn waffle bowls, for crying out loud," as my husband had put it. Was it time for treats already? Were we going to wrap up hours before fireworks (I assumed there would be some, somewhere) and fireflies (because, obviously)?

"Mmmm. Thanks," Paul said, already taking a bite.

"Yuck. Aren't there cupcakes or ice cream or som'in?" Jacob asked.

"Shut up, you whiny little brat," Summer said.

"Summer!" Sam warned.

I tried to focus on the taste of fresh berries, which made up for the canned whipped cream I normally didn't buy. But there was something in the air.

"Ms. Van and I have to run an errand," Abby said.

"There's nothing open," Summer said. "Are you going to get gas or something?"

"Hey Summer Ruth. Let's go see if the fish are biting

better." Ah. Paul might have still been on the new side, but he knew how to read all the signs.

Summer sulked behind him, thankfully knowing better than to argue, and Jacob followed, likely bored of us already or maybe just to argue over the fishing rods. Sam came outside then, followed by a sulky Bradford. Baylor?

"Are you really gonna go chasing her? You know where she is."

"Benji—" *Benji!* "I heard your opinion. I don't need to hear any more, papi!"

"Van, shouldn't we take Ben with us?" Abby asked calmly.

"I can come, too," Sam said.

"Um, should I leave or…?" *What the hell is going on?* is what I wanted to ask. And climb into that gazebo and not give a dang about any of it was what I wanted to do. Alas.

Abby and Van exchanged another glance. Van nodded. I felt like I was in seventh grade and my parents were talking in code about something my crazy Aunt Judy did. Van nodded.

"Evie has been sneaking around with a real di… um… bad news kinda guy," Abby explained, as though I actually was one of the children. "It's been a struggle, and she is supposed to be hanging out at Van's brother's today, but he just called and said –"

"He went to pick her up and she was already gone. I'm so stupid!" Van snapped. "That child is a wonderful liar, and she learned from the best. Me! I should never have left before Mick came to get her!"

"Van, you're not stupid. Teenagers, by nature, are the worst. Sorry, Ben." I hid my smile at Sam's words. Let him be the calmer and encourager. I could go inside and –

"Do you want me to drive you guys?" Sam continued. "Ben, do you want to stay here—"

"Mami!" Ben's voice suddenly held life. "I'm coming with you. I told you I know where she is!"

"Yeah, yeah. Of course. Come on."

Ben's face had morphed from surly to panicked in a matter of moments. Oh, the precious hearts of adolescent boys trying to be big, strong men could do me in. I wanted to put a fortifying arm around him, as I am sure his Granny Fi did often.

I smiled as Sam did just that. "I'll drive, you guys. Really. Let's go." He turned to me. "Mama, the kids…"

"I know, babe. Go on."

I watched them get in the car and drive off, thinking of my own days raising two teenage girls. Honestly, it wasn't all that bad for me. Paul, on the other hand, had his youngest daughter and his Mustang sneak outta town for sunny California without a glance back. Sometimes, when he and Katy verbally sparred, I could tell he was still a little scarred from it. I couldn't wait to tell him that our *alone time* was going to be delayed a little longer.

"Where does a teenage girl get lost in a place like this?" Paul asked. "Never mind. I heard it. And I don't wanna know."

He looked from the porch to the creek, where Summer was wading while Jacob fished and *both* of them were singing "So, why can't you see-e-e you belong with me-e-e?" at the top of their lungs. "God help me. We both have served our time with daughters, but what about Summer and Josie and Vivi and Lexie? And there could be more. I don't know how many teenage girl seasons I have in me."

"That's an irrelevant pondering," I said, reaching for his hand. "You have to stay in it with me. And to answer, incidentally, the number will be countless in that it will *always* be growing, Father Abraham. Descendants numbered like the stars."

"I hope she stays like this," he said, nodding at my granddaughter. "She's the next to be a teenager, so let's just freeze time."

We both knew that was impossible, but three July Fourths before, I'd have said the same about someday sharing my first granddaughter with a husband and a patriarch who wasn't Randall. *Impossible* had been rendered nearly meaningless.

I squeezed his hand. "We can try."

We watched them in silence for, oh, I don't know, seventeen seconds (maybe seven minutes, but still), before my phone rang. I had forgotten to turn down the ringer. Apple is always changing those volume settings on me, and everything was still quite loud from the Cooking Music (aka Tom Petty with a side of Alice in Chains) playlist I'd been blasting in the kitchen. The jarring sound seemed to wake Paul just as it startled me almost out of my seat.

"Mama?"

It was Sam.

"Yep?" I couldn't help feeling mildly panicked for multiple reasons. One, they hadn't been gone long. Two, I was prone to anxiety. Three, a mid-day call just a few years earlier had alerted me to my husband's death and maybe I'd never get over that.

"Are y'all still at the cabin?"

"Yep." I almost exhaled. He sounded fine, albeit a little irritated.

"So, Evie was not at the house where Ben said she would be. At least, there weren't any cars and no one answered the door. We have two more places to check."

"Okay…" I mean, I was concerned for Evie, but I didn't really require a play by play.

"One is on this side of town, and one is closer to Helen, so we were wondering…"

I closed my eyes. Helen was more than a half hour away, not a big deal when it wasn't a holiday, and we weren't in unfamiliar mountain roads. Still, there was no way I could say no, even with the distinct possibility – no, fact – that I was about to royally piss of my husband and for that matter, my grandkids.

"I guess, Sam. Send it to me."

Paul stood up as I read the texted directions. "Where are we going?"

He didn't even look aggravated. Maybe my sense of adventure (a therapist once called it *co-dependency in disguise*) had rubbed off on him.

"Toward Helen. This guy she's been chasing works at the caramel corn place."

He gaped at me. "Not to be confused with the regular popcorn place?"

I stared right back at him and deadpanned, "Exactly. Sam is adamant on that point."

Paul open his mouth and then closed it several times. I was trying not to laugh at the absurdity of the whole thing.

"And what are we supposed to do if we see her there? Citizen's arrest?"

I scraped the toe of my Converse along the planks of

the porch, looking down. "Eat some caramel corn and wait for further instruction."

"Well, as long as there are snacks. Let's get to it."

"I don't even like caramel corn. I thought we were doing s'mores again tonight."

"Jacob, I promise you I heard you say that the first three times."

It was unlike Paul to be short with *my* grandson, even though Jacob had morphed more comfortably than his older brother or Summer into being *ours*.

Jacob harrumphed. I turned the music up.

"Jess. Please."

"You don't even like Sting?" Sure, "Fields of Gold" wasn't exactly a rollicking summer anthem, but I'd always loved the poetry of it.

"I like it," Summer said. "Turn it up louder, Mimi. Daddy sings this one sometimes."

Because I used to sing it to him, I thought mournfully. I didn't turn it up, just turned around to look at Sam's little mini and only daughter, and before I could drink in her gold-flecked eyes and wavy brown locks, I turned back around to blink back my tears.

Will you stay with me? Will you be my love? Not the most profound lyrics ever, but they were suddenly landing on my heart like arrows. I wanted to squeeze Paul's hand, but in that moment, what I really wanted was Randall's hand, and thus the constant underlying complication in life reared again.

"Mimi, will you change the station?" At least Jacob had

changed his tune.

"Yes, Mimi," Paul echoed. "Please, God, change the station."

For once, I didn't answer. I wanted to hear the damn song, and it wasn't hurting anyone, and these two boys could wait fifty more seconds. Paul started drumming the fingers of his right hand on the gear stick. Jacob kept whining. Summer started singing louder. So I harmonized and looked out the window and thought of a far-off time when Randall's arm was around me while I held Summer the first time she spent the night at our house, and we oohed and ahhed over her chubby, pink, four-month-old cheeks, and when she screamed for the first half hour, we sang "Roll With It, Baby" to her and to each other.

I thought those were the happiest days of my life, yet every year, every season, I found myself waiting. I was always waiting for the next thing, the next endeavor, the next challenge, the next joy. Was I ever truly joyful? Was I never satisfied?

I looked ahead and saw we were almost to the little Bavarian downtown where we'd be searching for a teenage girl I'd met once and, apparently, caramel corn.

"Paul—"

My next words were cut off by the loudest smack I'd ever heard, the nightmarish sound of metal on metal, of something moving hitting something that should be immovable, of Paul's guttural yell and the kids' terrified shrieks. It seemed like I should be screaming, too, but I had no breath, none at all. Paul had been knocked toward me and then back, captured by the G-force and his seatbelt. I was thrown to the right and then the left, and then I saw blood.

IT HAD BEEN A WHILE SINCE SHE CLOSED A PLACE DOWN. Moving back near her Daddy and sisters meant there were more watchful eyes on her, more daily check-ins, and all of that also meant she heard Mama's voice in her head more than she did when she was living an hour up the road. So she didn't stay until last call, leaving all the money she made at any given gig right there at the bar, talking to guys who looked good at best but were rarely what Mama would call *worthy*, turning on her charm, or just as often, wasting time. The past weeks, back home, she'd had dinners with Daddy and Jessie or over at Danielle's house or out with Julie. On the nights she didn't, she was first watching Salty Lips practice and then being part of it, hanging with Brit, getting to know El, sleeping with him. It was a fast transition, and she was enjoying it more than she enjoyed anything about the life she'd left behind in Wilmington.

This night was different; the third of July seemed to leave a sparkle in the air, an energy that was fraught with possibility. People were off the next day, the weather was Surfside-summer perfect (she personally believed Ed Piotrowski probably controlled the weather), the show had been, admittedly, great, and everyone who remained was riding the vibes. Brittney was still behind the bar, and now Katy had El behind her, a hand on the small of her back, and Harrison next to her, his face morphing between dark and brooding (which was, in Katy's opinion, the usual) and smiling rather smolderingly at Brittney.

My new stepsister and me, dating hot, rock band brothers. This could be a rom-com. Or an absolute disaster.

"Did she make you one of these?" Harrison said, a little slur in his voice as he held up a tumbler of a half-gone something. He turned to Mikey and Ringo, who were on the other side of him caught up in their own nonsensical discourse about a bar down the road who kept getting their outdoor stage shut down. "She's a genius, my girl. Had this gig for five minutes and already the best in town."

"Shush," Brittney gushed, leaning way over the bar to kiss him. "You don't want to make the others jealous."

"Is that an old fashioned?" El asked his brother. "Are you a seventy-five-year-old accountant now?"

"Hey!" Brittney answered. "I have to practice. Because sometimes, we get *one-hundred-and-five-year-old* accountants."

"Well, then practice on me and make a Negroni."

She glared at him. "No one is ordering *that* here."

"You don't know." El pretended to sulk.

Katy rolled her eyes and asked for another Corona.

"What time are you gonna get off?" she asked Brittney.

She shrugged. "I think we stop serving at two. But I have a feeling if there are still people here, Ed will want to keep going. You guys could play another set!"

"God, no," Katy said as El added, "Nah. This crowd will be gone in the next hour."

"And Ringo can't lift his sticks anymore," Mikey chimed in.

"The hell I can't," Ringo grunted. "Cut this boy off. He's making less sense than usual."

Haha. They kept going. It was past midnight, and Katy was starting to feel as woozy as the rest of them looked, but she wasn't sure she could ask El to leave.

"You guys don't have to stay until I'm done," Brittney said. "Harrison is waiting." He gave a completely out-of-character, drink-induced smile at that. "Obviously, I will be driving us to the condo. You're cut off, mister."

"Oh, come on, Buttercup. We have the whole day to recover tomorrow."

He has a point. Katy batted her eyes at El. "We do, too, I reckon," she said. "You ready to get a head start or—"

At that moment, a few iconic bars came over the speakers. El batted *his* eyes right back at her and took her hand. "One dance," he said, and that was all she needed to hear. She set her bottle on the bar and followed him to the dance floor underneath the towering oak and the bazillion fairy lights. Don Henley started singing of empty roads and beaches. El had The Salty Lips learning The Ataris' version of the song, but right there, with her in his arms, he was softly singing the words in their classic form, with no growl or edge to his voice. She was melting.

As "The Boys of Summer" progressed into its speedier

cadence and more urgent lyrics, they danced a little faster, too. El's hands on her waist, her hands on his shoulders, neck, chest, whatever she could reach at the moment. He was a much better dancer than she was, and all she really wanted to do was stand still, touch him, and hear him sing those words right into her ear. El read her body language and stopped the dance. He kissed her neck with his open mouth and then led her by the hand back to the bar to close their tab and collect their things.

Harrison was now nursing a Coke and smiled a bit more clear-eyed at them. "See you tomorrow?" he said, and El hugged him. Katy felt a surge of warmth. The two brothers had only recently started mending their fractured relationship after years of shared childhood trauma and a tragic separation neither of them talked about and neither she nor Brittney fully knew about.

Katy winked at Brit and linked her arm through El's as they walked to the parking lot. She'd wedged her Mustang in between El's big ol' truck and another oak tree. He walked her around to her driver's door and there it was.

Under the window, the entire "white platinum" door was covered in brand new art: the word TRASH was keyed into paint, the "T" so deep that there was little hope of ever fixing it. Katy should know; she had keyed a car, maybe two, in her lifetime.

"Mother fu—" El started, and Katy quickly cut him off.

"Bitches have nerve," she said. "I absolutely did *not* see this coming."

"What the hell?!" El exclaimed. "We are thirty years old. Atalaya is *married*. What are they thinking about? If Ed's cameras reach this far, we are publishing this everywhere. *Everywhere!*"

Katy snorted. Tears ran down her face. She was laughing hard enough to bring tears, but crying, too. There was no way she could afford to fix this mess. She walked around to the other side, grateful to find it unharmed. Who would have thought the White Walkers would pull something like this?

El was angrily scrolling through his phone. "What are you going to do?" Katy asked. "Tell on her?"

"Well." He stared at her thoughtfully for a moment. "Yes. But also, I was going to call the police."

She rolled her eyes. "They don't care about this. There is no way we can prove who did it. No one will believe a hometown *darling* had anything to do with—"

"Sweetness, we have to make a police report for your insurance, if nothing else."

Oh Lord. He is so cute. She stifled more drunken laughter. "That would imply I have comprehensive on this old girl, El, which I absolutely do *not*. And you siccing Horry County's finest on them is not the answer."

"Then what is, Kakes?"

This was not her first rodeo with the likes of a heifer like Atalaya. All the possibilities for retribution clicked through her head, but El was not the person to help her choose. "Hmph," she said, and beckoned him to follow her as she went half-stomping, half-galloping back to the bar to tell Brittney what happened.

"Oh, hell no!" Brittney untied her apron and tossed it to Ed. "I'll take you up on your offer," she said to him. And then to the guys, "Can one of you drive Harrison home? I need to go with my sister."

Ringo nodded slowly. "Where *you* going?"

El started shaking his head as Katy and Brittney answered in a flurry of responses. His drummer shrugged.

"All I got was the car was keyed and '162.50.'"

"BAIL MONEY!" Mikey yelled. "We're going with you! Who's driving?!"

"Not any of you," El said.

"I'm totally fine," Brittney said. "Let's *roll!*"

Katy led the charge back to the parking lot, feeling like a teenager – for better or worse – as her hodge-podge-entourage followed behind. "El! Keys!" Brittney directed, and she jumped into the driver seat of his truck with Harrison at shotgun and Katy, after El refused to let Mikey ride in the cargo bed, smushed in the backseat with one, two, three grown-ass music men.

"It says 'Trash.'" Ringo observed as the truck started rolling.

"Thank you, Sir Obvious," El said, as Katy responded with, "No shit."

"So where are we going?" Ringo asked. Katy found herself wondering again how old he was and why in the world he was involving himself in their shenanigans.

"First, to Dollar General," Brittney said. Mikey let out a woop.

"I know you ain't doin' what I think you're doing."

"What are you guys talking about?" El asked.

He hadn't grown up where Katy had, but Brittney had, and clearly Mikey had. They needed eggs and toilet paper. This was war.

"But we don't even know where they're staying," El said.

"We'll find 'em. All we have to do is drive up and down the boulevard until we find the Ho-Mobile."

"How do you know what she drives?" Ringo asked.

Katy turned to him. "Just got a text from my friend at Horry County dispatch. We have make, model, and plates."

Ringo's face melted into laughter. He turned to El.

"These two ain't playing. You and your brother better watch out."

"When did you have time to do that?"

Katy was furiously pounding letters into her phone. "While we were getting in."

Mikey let out another woop. El gave him a swift elbow and told him to shut up.

"Brit, do you think your little Chamber friend is involved? I don't want to burn your bridges."

Brittney shook her head. "Light the match. If she was involved, IDGAF how she feels about any of this."

"Let me tell you how I feel about this," Harrison grumbled.

The car got quiet for a second. "Eh, screw it," he finally added. "Let's toss some eggs."

That time, everyone joined in the hollers. Katy was practically sitting on El's lap, and though they were almost to the store, she settled in against his arm, feeling outraged and silly and embarrassed and exhilarated all at once – and happy to be anything but bored.

Two hours later, filled with sobering Cook Out milkshakes and Cokes, everyone got back into their own cars and headed in their own directions. Katy followed El home– *to his home, not really hers, was it?*

It was a short drive, and once he backed into the

driveway and shut off the engine, he quickly walked to her ruined door and scowled at it.

"So tired," he said, loudly enough for her to hear clearly.

She couldn't pick out any emotion in his voice. Was he mad at her? Did he find her ridiculous? Was he regretting not being with a more refined idiot like Atalaya?

"Yep," she said in a voice that was too quiet and didn't sound like hers.

She sat there in a bit of a panic. Before she could register it, he was opening her door.

"Ready for bed?"

She stepped out and looked him in the eye.

"Was tonight… was this too much for you?"

"What?" he said. "You mean the teenage mutant ninja hijinks?"

"I guess…"

He smiled, but not with his eyes. "It's not the way I would have handled it, but… it was pretty fun."

She didn't know what to say.

"I respect that it sent Atalaya a direct, mostly non-physically threatening message," he continued. "But it won't fix your car. And if that beach house has cameras…"

"Ringo said it didn't."

"Ringo was at least half-baked."

She giggled. "Who wasn't?"

He gave her his hand and led her up the stairs.

They showered in separate bathrooms. She wore actual pajamas, well, an old Pelicans tee-shirt and some shorts. She wasn't expecting much when she opened the door to El's bedroom. He was already asleep. Ignoring the pounding in her chest, and that familiar voice of Mama's in her head saying, *Katy, you have got to grow up and handle things with sense or this boy is going to walk straight away,* she slid next to him and drifted quickly into sleep.

Jessie

"Mɪᴍɪ!"

I couldn't tell whose voice was calling, and the sobbing from the backseat jolted me. I couldn't turn my neck; my seatbelt had locked and also, my neck felt a little like my head had been screwed on too tight.

"Babies!" I managed. "Are you okay? Are you both okay?"

"Ye-e-es…" Summer wailed, while Jacob very brokenly said, "NO!"

Paul's seatbelt unlocked. I couldn't turn my head to see him, or maybe I could but didn't want to. He had to be okay if he was moving, right?

"Jess? Can you move?"

I tested my neck again. It gave a little. My head pounded. My side twinged. But everything else seemed fine. "Yeah. Just…"

He reached over and released my seatbelt. His forehead was bleeding above his left eye. He looked alien to me, scared, disheveled. Paul was never disheveled.

"The kids…"

"I got 'em."

"Paul, are you okay?"

"Yeah," he answered abruptly, shaking his caved in door, jarring it lose. In seconds he had opened the back one, and Jacob sprung into his arms. Summer had already gone out her door and was yanking on mine.

"Careful, Baby," I said, but there was no way she could hear me. Jacob's cries were frighteningly loud. She threw herself at me, and I was at once thankful she was mobile and nervous I'd cracked a rib. She didn't hear my gasp over her own crying. I squeezed her as tightly as I could. What the hell had just happened?

Paul ambled over to our side of the car, Jacob's lanky legs dangling nearly to the ground, through Paul had a tenuous hold on him and Jacob's arms were squeezing Paul's neck like a vice. I hoped his neck didn't feel like mine, but based on the look of his head and, oh my God, the driver's side door, I was certain my husband was probably hurt.

That is when my breath caught up with me, and I started to shake with my efforts not to cry.

Summer's feet were on the ground, but she leaned fully into my chest. Paul managed to put Jacob down and he lunged for his sister. I couldn't brace myself for it and the blow jarred my ribs. *Holy shit.* And Paul, standing behind them, caught my eye over the top of the kids' heads. Blood and water mingled in a stream down his face.

"We should get out of the car," I managed. Paul put a hand on Jacob's back and helped coax the kids off of me.

"Get on the grass," he said, in that way daddies have that is equal parts authoritatively gruff and steeped in compassion. They obeyed. He held his hand out to me and helped me up, my whole upper body protesting at the movement and my brain forbidding me to look in his eyes.

"Jess—"

"I'm okay," I said, with certainty but not nearly as much gentleness that I wanted to convey in the moment. I just… couldn't.

"I have to call Sam," I said.

"Jess." He squeezed my hand really tightly. I forced myself to look.

"Are you okay?" I was going to lose it, and I wanted so much not to.

He answered that question and the ones I didn't ask with, "We'll be fine."

He told the kids to stay with me and walked to the car to assess the driver, who had, from my best guess, tried to pass us as she turned onto the road and instead, creamed us.

I sat in the grass. My neck was loosening up. My left side throbbed when I inhaled, but I was trying to breathe deeply anyway to calm the inner chaos. Jacob sat between my legs and lay his head on me. He had a cut nearly identical to Paul's on his forehead, though thankfully smaller, and he was still crying in gasps. Summer sat next to me and handed me my phone. I don't know where I'd had it in the car or where she'd gotten it; in that moment, I just thanked the Lord that our precocious girl wanted to be a grown up, because I could certainly use another one in that moment.

I dialed, and Sam picked up on the first ring, certainly

assuming we had news of Evie.

"Sam? We're okay," I said. And then I handed the phone to Summer as my own sobs escaped.

"Are we still going to the popcorn place?"

Paul, sitting on the edge of the cot that Jacob had just jumped from, ruffled his hair. "Caramel corn, buddy. And I expect that maybe… well…" He looked at me, seated in a chair across from him. "I don't know. We can probably do whatever you want at this point."

Sam and Summer appeared in the doorway of our little curtained cubicle. "Verdict?" he asked.

"Sore as hell," Paul answered. "Three stitches. Probable concussion. And your mama has whiplash, either bruised ribs or pulled muscles, nothing broken."

Jacob, whom Sam had released to us while he went to take care of the paperwork, walked up to his daddy and pouted. "Why couldn't I get any stitches?"

"Sorry not sorry, bud," Sam said, putting a firm hand on Jacob's shoulder and looking like he wanted to scoop him up like a baby. "Just a little glue for you. Glue is kinda cool."

Summer giggled at that, and then so did Paul. He was probably a little punch drunk after the blur of the last two hours. Our Jeep was probably totaled. The driver of the other car, thankfully a Honda Civic and not one of the typical massive bro-trucks that were all over the road, was a teenage girl who cried harder than the kids and I put together. Thankfully, her mama showed up five minutes after the accident or I would have pulled her into my lap, too.

We weren't sure how we would get home from Georgia in another day. We weren't sure if Abby and Van had gotten to Evie yet. They had come straight to the accident site from somewhere on the other side of Blairsville. Around the time Jacob was patched up, and he and Summer were declared good to go, Van got a text from one of Evie's friends, back toward Blairsville again. We all assured Abby it was okay, and she rode alone with Van and Ben. That was before we knew the paramedics would insist that Paul and I be seen at the hospital – 20 more miles away in a different direction. Sam and the kids followed in an Uber.

Through the years, Randall and I had spent literally thousands of dollars on cookouts and holiday accouterments and fireworks; this, however, would be the most expensive Fourth in my life.

So we weren't sure what to do now that it was past six o'clock on the Fourth of July and at least two of us felt like we, well, got hit by a car.

"What are the odds of getting a ride all the way back to Blairsville?" I asked no one in particular.

"Abby is on her way," Sam said, matter-of-factly and as though I should have known.

"How many times are they driving back and forth?" I asked, like it mattered, like I wouldn't do the same thing for one of my kids and like I wasn't so proud and thankful for how Abby was trying to help everyone.

"Did they get Evie?" Summer asked.

"Do we get to see fireworks?" Jacob asked.

"Can I take a nap here until Abby comes?" Paul asked.

Sam looked at me.

"Don't look at me," I said, enjoying the effects of the muscle relaxer I'd been given. "I have no clarifying details, answers, or plans."

"She doesn't even have a *pla*—," Summer chimed in, quoting a favorite scene from *Friends*.

"But we have to see fireworks! It's the Fourth of July!" Jacob argued.

I closed my eyes, my head back against the chair, and let my son deal with his son. Normally, I would have been worried sick about Paul and the kids and Abby *and* Van and her kids, but all of that was zapped and drained right out of me. I didn't want to think about anyone, because my brain would inevitably rewind to the sound and feel of the accident, and that…

Well, I hated to admit defeat, ever, for any reason. But just then, it was too much.

"This was *unadvisable*," Paul said in my ear. I'm not even sure how I heard him. The colorful explosions in the sky were booming every twenty seconds, and there was a marching band keeping a steady beat in my temples on top of that. Cyclobenzaprine apparently did not work on the brain. Jacob was a happy boy, but Paul and I were barely hanging on.

Could we have argued? Probably. We were sexagenarians fresh from the E.D., after all. But would we? – after Abby drove her SUV to get us with Van's parents following, bringing us homemade quesitos for comfort and gratitude. Fiona and her husband, Valentín, offered to take Paul and me back to our cabin so the kids could stay and enjoy the festivities. Oh, the offer was so inviting. We both absolutely wanted to leave. But neither of us mustered the strength to say yes. We just sat on two lawn chairs in the square, ate our sweet, cheesy, still-warm pastries, and shut our mouths. It was the easiest response.

I always loved the fireworks. Well, truthfully, I had always loved the Fourth of July. Now, though? Even in the great *after*, when everything in our new life needed to be re-established, cobbled together, redeemed, and/or created from scratch, this particular holiday held more weight than a day for cookouts and sparklers should. During our first summer together, Paul and I – no, not accurate— *me, myself, and I* tried to gather all of our kids together for something kind of traditional at my old beach house, the one I'd shared with Randall and tried to share with Paul. It was all too soon. It was an epic hot mess. I couldn't even stand to think about it.

The following summer, we were newly married – and I was newly diagnosed with uterine cancer.

Really, this one was probably the best of the three. The quesitos were really good, and none of us had died.

Even I could admit, the bar was set pretty low.

There was a small break in the explosions and some band started to play. I didn't notice myself drifting off until I felt a hand on my forearm. I jumped in my seat, and it hurt.

"Jessie? Would you and Paul like to leave before the finale? We can beat some of the traffic and avoid the… absolute fecking racket."

Fiona's gentle, rolling voice was a sharp contrast to the look of exasperation on her face and of course, her choice of very welcome words.

"Let's skedaddle," Paul said as he stood. He tapped Sam's shoulder, and Sam nodded his understanding, Jacob sitting in his lap in a sleepy but still mesmerized daze. Summer was sandwiched between them and Abby, who had Van, Ben, *and* Evie on the other side of her. I didn't have the crackling energy that I usually reserved for such up-close human drama, but I tucked away a whole list of questions to ask, tomorrow.

The ride back to the cabin took twenty minutes instead of thirty. I had my eyes closed the whole time, listening to the gentle lilt of Fiona combat the up-tempo, melodic Spanglish of Valentín. Once out of the congestion of the town square and back on to 348, they argued about Evie as though we were not in the backseat, or as though they didn't care.

"Van needs to get her in check. Enough of this woke parenting, being her friend. She is her mama. And Evie is a rebellious child. It's nothing a little spankability won't fix."

"She can't *spank* her. She is going on fifteen years old."

"She's a nena. She needs a mother. And a papa, for that matter."

"Well, Capitán, she doesn't have one. Not her real one and not a step one any time soon, and you really need to shut your gob about that, because if Van hears you, she will spiral and not speak to you. Teenage girls feel stupid feelings and react to them in stupid ways. Actually, remove 'girls' from that sentence. They are young. They will be stupid."

That last bit was like a prayer. I almost laughed, almost said "Amen,' but I was trying to be still and also to pretend like we couldn't hear a word they were saying. Everyone in the car had suffered a teenage runaway in some fashion. We all survived, and Van would, too.

We all survived. I swallowed a lump in my throat.

Pulling up to the cabin felt like breaking the surface after almost drowning. We said gracious thanks and good-byes, and wordlessly entered the house. I didn't look at the dishes in the sink or the remnants of the *start* of a fun afternoon; I just grabbed a water bottle and dragged myself up the stairs. I heard Paul, an absolute hero, preparing the coffee maker for the following morning. When he joined me, I was already in the shower, water and soap and tears converging down the drain. I could barely breathe.

He was next to me in seconds. This was an act, a scene, that love-crazed teens or the melty romances that inspired them would never get. We were dirty and stinky, weary and a little busted, having several layers of emotional breakdown. My make-up had long since disintegrated. Paul's hair smelled like air-bag ashes. I was wincing with every inhale, and he had an impressive shiner forming around his left eye.

We were a mess, and if I was assessing correctly, about to fall apart.

But we fell together. Frankly, it was how we had started. Unfortunately, it seemed like our default, too.

As I was gingerly lathering myself, still heaving a bit, not having any idea what to say, Paul started washing my hair. I didn't ask or expect it but letting him was easier. I closed my eyes as he firmly massaged my scalp and then gently, slowly lathered my long locks. The shower didn't have a telescopic shower head, so he turned me right around with my back to the water and made sure I was rinsed. I still didn't look at him, as I was still crying, and if he was too, I didn't think I would be able to stand it.

I wanted to return the gesture, but it hurt to raise my

left arm. I just waited while he repeated the process, swift-
ly but carefully avoiding his Saniplast bandage, on his own
hair. And then he turned the water off, stepped out, and
waited for me with one of the many fluffy towels stacked
on the linen cupboard, holding one hand out to steady me.
I grasped it, still avoiding his eyes, even while he wrapped
the towel around me and took another to dry my hair. I
kept trying to say something, just to thank him, just to
check on him, but fear held my tongue. I stood still as he
wrapped a towel around himself, and then finally, as he
faced me again and lifted my chin with one finger, I said
what I'd always said to him when I was without words:

"*Paul.*"

For my husband, the affirmation of his name – a name
he had changed himself when he was of legal age, gave
him comfort, just as the warmth of human connection
gave it to me.

I finally looked at him, and his green eyes were full, of
weariness, of sadness, and of other deep things I couldn't
quite label but recognized all the same.

He nodded at me with reassurance. We padded down
the hall to our room where we managed the minimum
tasks and articles of clothing. Paul insisted I needed to
prop myself up on a whole mountain of pillows, and
though it seemed like a fuss, once I nestled against them, I
could breathe more easily. He turned on the TV and found
the channel showing *Friends*. There always was one. I listened to him shake out some ibuprofen and gulp his water. *Probable minor concussion,* they'd said. He looked like it
was definite and big. He shut off the lamp.

"We shouldn't have gone to those fireworks," I finally
said. "How's your head?"

"No worse for the fireworks." He reached over and squeezed my hand.

"Paul…" I said one more time.

"Go to sleep, Jess," he said. Then he leaned over and kissed me, softly and quickly. "It'll keep." He burrowed back down in his own pillows. "It will all keep."

THE HOUSE WAS EERILY QUIET EVEN THOUGH it was later than usual when Katy woke up. Her room, well, El's room was gloriously dark and cold; he kept the air blasting like only a latchkey, broken-home Millennial who grew up without AC and now had some money would do. She knew if she opened the door, she'd be flooded with the mid-morning sun, as the living room and kitchen had plenty of windows and no coverings. But El had to be out there, and she wanted El.

Blinking her eyes to focus, she picked up her phone from the night stand. Texts from all the sisters, mostly from Brittney. One text from Daddy that oddly just read, "I love you." She'd have to come back to that. Missed call from Julie, who alternated days she called Katy and their older sister Danielle. *She probably calls both of us on holidays.* Since Julie got married, she had been trying to take up where Mama had left off, staying involved, keeping them linked. *Later, Jules.* There were a few messages on the band group text; she mostly wouldn't respond to those yet. They would play again tomorrow night and then *maybe* she would start to feel like one of them. Maybe.

She smiled as she ignored all of them and composed a message to El.

MORNING. BONUS POINTS IF YOU BRING COFFEE TO ME.

She added a few emojis to encode just how much she had enjoyed their night and hit send.

A telltale "ding" donged on the other side of the bed. *Oh.* Was El the last human in civilization who went to the bathroom in the morning without his phone? Was he like Daddy and reading the actual newspaper in there?

One more stretch and she jumped out of the bed.

"Good mooooorning!" she called into the living room. Silence met her.

She glanced down the hall to the bathroom door. It was open, the bathroom empty.

"El?" He wasn't in the kitchen either. Would he be in the other bathroom, with all Brittney's stuff in it?

Nope.

And not the porch either. Dang. It was already a scorcher out there.

Okay. Where in Hades does a guy go on a holiday morning with no phone? His truck was in the driveway. He wouldn't have walked to get bagels without it. She had butterflies in her stomach as she jogged back to the bedroom, telling herself not to do what she was on her way to do.

His phone screen, of course, was locked.

His wallpaper was The Salty Lips logo. She would have smiled at that. But all his missed messages were there. One from her. Three from the band. And eighteen –

– eight-*freaking*-teen–

from Ata-flippin-laya.

Aw. Hell. No.

Where IS he?

She unlocked her phone and dialed Brittney. She didn't have time for texts. Maybe Brit would know something. Or maybe Katy would sound like a psycho wannabe girlfriend.

Brittney didn't answer anyway.

Her total lack of ideas on what to do next was coupled by her need to pee. She stepped into the bathroom, flung herself onto the seat in an exasperated pout, and finished her business. It was only when she got her hands lathered and looked in the mirror that she saw it:

YOU LOOK PERFECT. MEET ME AT BEACH.

She immediately turned to fetch her suit; a ridiculous smile plastered on her face.

Ten minutes later, red bikini and waterproof mascara in place, she walked in the opposite direction of the beach to Benjamin's for two iced coffees, lotsa cream lotsa sugar-free s'mores syrup. She munched ravenously on a giant cinnamon roll while she waited in the crowd. She also looked around for any white walkers present. She guessed they might still be dealing with the eggy, wet toilet paper-y mess in the front yard of their rental, which was on the very south side of Garden City Beach, not really in the breakfast radius for this café, but one never knew.

Ick. It made her mad all over again to think about her ruined door. Short of ordering one of those stupid car magnets (advertising what?) to cover most of it, she had no idea what to do. The boys had given plenty of suggestions during their joy ride last night, but Katy just laughed at them. Her paycheck lent itself to some fun extras, like the stuff she was currently waiting for, but she had no margin for whatever a replacement would cost. Asking Daddy was her only other option. And oh, how she did *not* want to do that.

She said a cheery goodbye to Tyler as he handed her the drinks and walked in double time down the road, making it to the beach in less than fifteen minutes. The sun was out, and sweat was soaking her hair and décolletage. She giggled out loud; Mama would be so proud of her using that flowery phrase instead of "boob sweat."

There was all kinds of sweat by the time she reached the First Avenue beach access and then fought through eighty-zillion umbrellas to look for El in *his* spot (their spot), with a great view of the pier and not too far from Neal and Pam's in case they had a corn dog emergency. She saw a small group of moms with little kids she recognized from church, making up a small city block with their pails and blankets and inflatables and coolers. *Let me walk waaaaay around that.* Then she saw Santa Greg from Murrells Inlet and his girlfriend Nancy, decked out in red and flanked by more children. They were so fun, and she'd have to stop and say hello later. Then she saw the lead singer of Jeremy's Ten, the Pearl Jam cover group that El loved to open for; well, they only did it once, but he had high hopes for another chance. Deron was sitting on his surfboard, surrounded by his four magically gorgeous kids. Katy had met the Hunter clan last time they came to the beach, and especially when they were surfing, they looked more like faery folk than human. El was parked next to them, sipping water, chatting it up. He'd spread a real red-and-white checked blanket out in front of him, flanked with a speaker, a cooler, and fold-up beach table set for two. He was laughing and engaging but looking over his shoulder every few seconds.

He's looking for me.

Suddenly, Katy did not care about who she ran into or how cool versus dorky she looked. She took off at a run toward him, the coffees splish-splashing a little. He saw her and stood up, and when she reached him, she thrust the cups into Deron's hands and jumped right up into El's arms.

It was already a scorching day, so in spite of El's picnic setting, they drank their coffees while standing in the shallow water; the water was tepid, not cool, but as therapeutic as Katy needed. She relished the feel of the waves washing over their feet as they parked themselves amongst the thousands already gathered for a magical holiday.

"I was a little freaked out when I woke up." Katy asked. "Why didn't you bring your phone?"

El smiled alluringly. "I wanted you to find me," he said. "And I want nothing to do with messages, at least for the morning."

"I can appreciate that," Katy said, even though her nerve receptors twitched for her phone when it was more than two feet away for more than two minutes. All the female voices in her head yelled at her for that. *Live in the moment.*

"I did take a risk that you'd sleep all morning, though," he continued, his hand on the small of her back in a way that sent very different electric currents through her. "…especially after the night we had."

She snickered. "What a night." Egging a house was the opposite of sexy, but she found herself having no regrets.

"Not exactly what I had in mind for staying up extra late," he said. He bent his head to kiss her, a soft, coffee-flavored brush on her lips. "But it was fun."

"It *was* fun," she agreed. *You sound like a moron.* Why was she so disarmed around him? Where was all her wit and charm?

"And no cops at the house this morning, so there's that."

She grinned. "I expect they're busy with other things this morning. The golf cart parade starts soon."

El shook his head. "I will never understand."

"Are you kidding? I love it. My Nana and Poppa used to do it every year. Sometimes Julie and I would dress up and sit in the back and throw candy."

"Of course you did," he said. "What did you dress up as?" Another kiss. "A sparkler? Lady Liberty?"

"Hmmm." She relished his lips. "I was a Marine once. Wore Poppa's jacket. Sometimes we just did the red, white, and blue thing. Mama always got us some kind of patriotic wear, even if it was just the Old Navy matching t-shirts. But my favorite…" She trailed off teasingly.

He raised an eyebrow, waiting her out.

"Wonder Woman," she said. "Complete with boots."

"Aw, yes!" He wrapped her up in a hug and rocked her back and forth. "Can we recreate it for next year?"

Next year. She had never dated a guy for more than a few months. She had never wanted to.

"Absolutely!" she said. "But only if you're Captain America."

Another kiss. "I'll be whatever you ask."

Everything from her head to her toes tingled. "Well, since you were already my chef this morning, let's go eat."

They walked back to their spread. El opened the cooler and removed a container of avocado toast and another of sliced strawberries. Katy clapped her hands, ravenous, but kissed him again before they tucked in. They recounted the highs and lows of their set the night before, and what they would change for the next night, and then El borrowed a surfboard and went out to try a few waves while Katy shared her strawberries with Deron's youngest, Vivien. If the other kids were faery folk, Viv was their warrior-princess. She was what adults call precocious, maybe enchanting, occasionally delightful; Katy had gotten a lot of that when she was a kid. But a better word for it was so badass and in charge of your own self that it scares the crap out of some of the adults around you. Viv was blessed and lucky she had a cool family.

And even though she didn't see it at the time, she had been, too. It took her years to get it, how Mama tried to refine her, how Daddy tried to protect her, but they never stopped loving her, loving the spark in her, and neither did her sisters. They might not have always *enjoyed* her little-extra-sumthin'-sumthin', but they didn't deny its existence, which is more than what she could say for a long string of disappointing boyfriends and friends and bosses.

El made her feel like she was on a new trajectory, and it was no longer a string, but a rope.

"This was excellent."

Katy leaned back into El, sitting between his legs, the scents of salt and sweat, sunscreen and hot dogs wafting through the air. It was perfectly dusk, and they had literally played all day. They surfed a little with the Hunters, though Katy spent more time falling down and laughing than anything else. They got into a frisbee game with a family visiting from, where else, New Jersey. (Honestly, the *where else* could have been New York, West Virgina, or Ohio, as a tenth of each state seemed to be represented right there.) They took turns running across the street to Neal and Pam's for provisions; this time, she had the dang cheeseburger and El seemed to enjoy watching her polish off every last bite. Mikey and his girlfriend stopped by for a while. Katy talked to both her sisters: Danielle's family was hanging out with Mikayla's (Brittney's older sister), Julie and Robin ran some kind of race that morning, though Katy didn't know if that meant they physically raced the course or were in charge of the whole thing. It was all weird to her, and she couldn't keep track of Julie's endless goals.

She finally talked to Daddy that afternoon, sitting there with El's head on her lap while she tried to eat a cone from Drippy's before it melted all over him. She offered to drive to Georgia to go collect him and Jessie and gave a silent sigh of relief that she wasn't required. The irony of her ruined Mustang was not lost on her, and all she needed was to add post-traumatic stress to Daddy's concussion.

She put all the other feelings she had about Daddy and

Jessie being in a car accident deep into their own compartment. Today was not the day for those.

Just when she started to wonder if they should call it a day, Brittney and Harrison showed up, their arms laden with beach chairs, their own cooler, and a take-out bag from Mulberry Street.

"Aaaaaall we have done today is eat!" Katy said, jumping up from her own chair to hug Brit. "That is a statement of fact, not a complaint," she added.

"What do we have here?" El stood beside her and automatically put his arm around her waist. "It smells way better than we do at this point."

"Ew," Brittney said, while she set down her chair. "It's slices from Mulberry Street. Pepperoni and hot honey."

"Thank goodness we're sweating," Katy said. "Gimme!"

Harrison shook his head with a forced smile on his face. Katy hadn't heard much from Brittney that day, but it sounded like his kids' cancelled trip had definitely taken a toll on his holiday mood. They all sat, and she and Brittney caught up while the brothers stuffed their faces.

"So, did you hear from Madison?" Katy finally asked. She'd been wondering all day, even though she tried to put it out of her head.

Brittney bit her lip.

"So, yes?"

"I mean… yes. Yes. She sent me a scathing text basically. Said they spent the entire morning cleaning up the yard. They had to do it all themselves because it was a holiday and no power washers were working." Any moment of guilt Katy might have been starting to feel disappeared at that moment. She doubled over laughing.

El chimed in at that point. "Sounds like the goal was

achieved," he said.

"Did *you* hear from her highness?" Brittney asked. Her friendship with El had started way before the Atalaya days; she was probably angrier about the car keying than Katy was.

Wait, no. No way.

El cleared his throat, giving Katy a glance before answering.

"I set my phone to do not disturb all morning. Even left it at home. And there were many, many, *many* messages when I checked this afternoon." Katy's heart leapt in anticipation.

She would try to play cool, but Brittney didn't care. "Okay. Whatever, Mr. Screen Time Allowance. Then what?"

"I was going to tell Katy once I had everything taken care of," he said, looking at Harrison this time. "Between the two of them, I won't be able to keep a thing quiet, ever."

Harrison shook his head. "You knew what you were getting into, man." He good naturedly rubbed Brittney's shoulder. "Fire and fire just make a bigger fire."

"Well said," Brittney mused as Katy said, "Hell yes." The sisters high-fived and then launched.

"So, El, seriously? What?" Brittney asked as Katy asked, "SO WHAT DID SHE *SAAAAAAY*?!"

El kept his eyes on Harrison as he answered. Katy would be getting real sick of all the brotherly head-shakin' if Harrison wasn't moving out of town.

"We're gonna get it fixed, Kakes. And she's gonna pay for it."

"Whaaaaat?!" she and Brittney shouted in unison.

"Sit down, you guys," Harrison said from his chair. He

was digging back into the pizza and seemed more light-hearted than when he'd arrived. "Or I am eating all of this."

Katy sat while answering, "The heck you are. El, how? How do you know she's gonna pay for anything? Did she admit to doing it?"

Brittney raised an eyebrow. "I can't imagine. Madison was so adamant that they had nothing to do with it that she was ready to 'file an affidavit,' which she probably can't even spell."

Neither can I, Katy thought.

"I told them Ed pulled the camera footage from the parking lot," El said.

"No way! Is he even there today?" Brittney asked.

"No way," El echoed. "I didn't even talk to him. But what I did have was Brody's phone number, which I'm sure she didn't expect. So I told her if she wasn't willing to have your car fixed, I'd ask her rich husband to put up the cash instead."

Harrison nodded, "That's solid work, El," while Brittney gaped at him and Katy asked, "Do you really have his number?"

"Absolutely," El said. "And I probably wouldn't use it, because I'm not interested in someone's martial drama, but she doesn't know that. And she's going to make a few calls tomorrow and get back to you, Brit, about where we can take Katy's car."

"Ick," Brittney said. "Why me?"

"Because I don't want anything to do with her, and you're my bestie, and neither of us wants Kakes to have to deal with her, either," he said, eyes twinkling.

Katy and Brittney smiled at each other and then back at El.

"This is a formidable bond, I think," Brittney said. "I'll handle Atalaya the sea monster. You can block her number, El. And you," she turned to Harrison, who peered at her from under the long, damp hair falling in front of his eyes. It appeared whatever she was going to say disappeared as he looked at her. In a softer tone, she said, "Happy Fourth of July." And she kissed him.

Katy looked away and back to El. "Thank you for… I mean, I really…"

He smiled at her so fully that she didn't feel disarmed or anxious. Just grateful.

"I really don't like needing help, and I hate asking for it, which is hilariously ironic because I've probably had more than most people. So… it's not only thank you for the help, but thank you for recognizing what *would* help and just… handling it."

He took her hands. "You're welcome. Let's help each other, okay? Because I agree about the bond: it can be a strong one, with the four of us, and the three of us, and right here between you and me.

A single firework crashed into the air, signaling the start of the main show, a well-timed, beautiful ending to a perfect summer day.

Jessie

I HAD NOTICED SOME TIME IN MY LATE for-
ties that something as simple as sleeping soundly could
have me completely furled in the morning, like rigor mor-
tis has set in. This knowledge prepared me approximately
eighty-five percent for how I felt the next morning. The
drug cocktail had worked magically on both of us until it
was time to wake up.

Facing the music meant more than shaking out the
seriously painful stiffness. I knew we had to give words to
the previous night before they festered in us.

"I thought I was so smart with the coffee last night,"
Paul said. "If I had any wits, I would have brought it up
here and set the timer."

"Your wits are basically sprained," I said, and I gave
him the biggest smile I could muster in gratitude for the
mug he handed me.

"That's for damn sure." He sank back into the bed, holding his own mug but negotiating with himself.

"You can go back to sleep," I said. "I don't think anything is going to happen quickly this morning."

"Not if we're in charge of it," he said. "But we're gonna have to figure out the Jeep situation."

"Good luck with that. It's a holiday."

"Jess, how hard did *your* head get knocked? Because it is most definitely not a holiday."

I supposed he was right, but the fifth of July had always felt like a holiday to me… before. Randall always took it off work. He traveled a lot when the kids were growing up, and the little extra summer staycation day was always welcome. We rarely travelled for it, and some people might have thought we were crazy for wanting to "holiday" in Myrtle Beach when it was overwrought with tourists. But we just thought it was fun. We didn't mind waiting in a long line for bagels at Benjamin's or ice cream at Painter's or walking all of our stuff to the beach so we wouldn't have to search for parking. As transplants – Randall called us *replants* – from the cold, grey north, living by the South Carolina coast just never lost its luster for us… and neither had the fifth of July.

Two years ago, Paul and I woke up in my old house together, the one that was across the street from the ocean, the one that Randall and I had meant to spend the rest of our lives in, and found out that his only brother, from whom he'd long been estranged, had died. And that day became its own *holy* day, as Paul laid out dark pieces of his childhood to me, but did so over pancakes at the pier, while feeding me watermelon in bed, while sitting on our porch listening to the waves. I would never forget it. The heaviness of our current morning reminded me of that day.

I took a long sip of hot coffee and finally let myself look at him, really exam my husband's face, bruised and definitely showing new signs of wear. Our first years together hadn't held any of the uphill battles that our younger, first-time newlyweddedness had. We had resources, income, flexibility, for the most part, no kids depending on us (for vital things, anyway). What we didn't have was the same stamina or the expanse of years ahead of us to course correct.

I stopped considering and instead wondered aloud. "Why do I feel like everything is very fragile this morning?" I asked.

Without missing a beat, Paul answered, "Do you want my entire list of reasons or just the categories?"

That was actually a good question.

I took a deep breath, which accentuated my need to eat and top off my medication. "I think first, I just want to know we are okay. You and me."

My hands were clutching the mug, but he pried one away and held it.

"We've been better," he said, his lips upturning slightly.

"Paul. *Really*."

"Jess, what can I say? It's laughable at this point."

I looked at my lap. "I'm not laughing," I muttered.

"Jessie…"

"It hurts to laugh," I continued.

"Are you actually whining right now?"

I really wanted to sigh, but it didn't seem worth the discomfort. "Works for Jacob."

"Jessie." He got off the bed, walked around to my side, and sat down facing me. "Of course, we're fine. Why wouldn't we be? *We* are one thing I'm not worried about."

I truly *had* wondered if we were on the instinctive same page in the aftermath of the accident. This shouldn't have surprised me; we were an absolute Mars and Venus when it came to emotional processing. But it's what I wanted, so his response felt like a blow, and my eyes filled. *Damn it.*

"Jess! Baby, what is it?"

I shrugged, feeling foolish and searching for my words. They usually came easily for me, and that morning they were making me chase them, seemingly in circles.

"I just… we… the accident… When Randall…"

His eyes darted sideways for just a moment when I said *Randall.* That felt like an intersection, maybe.

"I don't know how to say all the things I feel," I finally managed.

"Don't overthink it." His hands clasped one of mine again. "Jess, it was scary. So scary. To have the kids in the backseat. To have you next to me. It sure sounded and felt a lot bigger than it ended up being. God was holding us, and I'm mostly grateful and relieved today. Annoyed and sore, but so thankful."

"I… I know. I am all of those things, too."

"But I feel like you're not telling me something else. Did you invite that poor little teenage driver to come live with us or something?"

I blew my breath out in a laugh. That *did* sound like something I would do.

Fine. "Right before the accident," I started, looking away from him, "I was thinking of Randall. I mean, I know that's not scandalous. I was just… well… I was wishing for him, Paul. I was wishing he was in that car with the kids and me at that moment. I was wishing he was here for this season, with Sam moving away. I was wishing for an easier understanding than what you and I have, because my heart is absolutely breaking in a way I didn't expect and can't explain and don't really even want to. And then—"

My tears overflowed.

"And then we crashed and for a moment that can't be measured, you thought I was dead and now you feel guilty?"

I nodded emphatically, silently.

"Jessie Rose." In one of his manly, so-confident movements, he pushed my pillow palace away and made himself my fortress. His arms held me tightly, and he spoke right into my ear, not in a whisper, but in a bold voice.

"You can miss Randall every day. Every second. You don't need me to tell you that. I will never fill his shoes. But I am here, and I love you, and I love those kids, too. I'm not going anywhere. And we *are* okay. I'm going to be here with you for all of this. You don't have to explain or apologize. I promise."

After all we had been through since two years ago March the twelfth, I shouldn't need those affirmations from him. Maybe I didn't need them, but I wanted them so intensely that I felt like I had just been fed a feast after voracious hunger.

He pulled away enough to look at me. "Why would you not want to tell me that?"

I shook my head. "I know you're right. I don't know why—"

Caressing my forearms, he continued, "I forget sometimes that everyone isn't impervious to trauma."

I scrunched my face up at him. "What an odd thing to say. *No one* is 'impervious to trauma.'"

He shrugged, and took his embrace away, and it really pissed me off.

"Is that what you really think?" I asked.

"Is that what *you* really think?"

"Of course it is."

My face morphed into a gape.

"What?"

"Paul, I assume you mean impervious to the *effects* of trauma. The stress. Because no one can control the shit that happens to them."

"Sure. Yes, Jess. That's what I mean. Why are you getting upset about this?"

I felt my insides shaking a little bit. Why *was* I?

I clicked through the mental list of reasons I felt upset *and* angry *and* traumatized. We'd already covered most of them. The ones we hadn't felt unspeakable.

We sat in the silence, real silence that greatly contrasted the version we had at home. There was absolutely no traffic on the road outside. No ocean breeze. No incessant beeping of golf carts backing out of driveways. Loudest to me, there was no near-tangible anticipation of someone stopping by. I always felt it. Here for a moment, it was gone. Sam and Abby had said to call them when we were ready, and I knew they wouldn't rush us.

I was always rushing me, though.

I exhaled, somewhat painfully, back into the headboard. And I reached for his hand again.

"I'm not impervious," I finally said. "I can't think about all the layers of last night without thinking about all the layers of March twelfth, and I can't think about July fifth without thinking of you and Charlie and all the things you went through before we ever got to March twelfth. And then I think about those dates a year from now, and what they could have looked like, and what they might look like, and my nerves explode, and Paul—"

He was encircling me again. I lay my head on his ample shoulder. I didn't want him to feel broken, even if I did. And me admitting I was didn't make me weak.

"I just forgot for a moment," I finally said, trusting that he knew what I meant. "And even though there are things I wish were different, I will never not want you right here where you are."

Holding me tight was his only response, and it was enough.

NEAL'S CREEKHOUSE WAS PACKED. WHEN THE Fourth was on Friday, the whole weekend felt like a continuous day. Katy found herself caught up in it, feeling downright sparkly. She was in front of the stage talking to Daddy's old friends, Richard and Brenda, who were die-hard music fans and promised her they weren't gonna miss many chances to see Paul's little girl playing. She smiled at that. Maybe she would make him proud after all.

Brit worked the Fishwalk's dayshift, and now she was there amongst the other Inlet industry workers who slung food and drinks or sundries or golf cart rentals all day and still wanted to enjoy the trappings of their tourist town at night. Katy watched her and Harrison feeding hush puppies to each other. The next weekend, he would be moving away, Brittney would be moving to her own place, and everything would be different. They were definitely making the most of this time; Katy wasn't always sentimental, but she recognized magic when it was happening.

Before the soundcheck, she had asked Ringo a whole list of questions about specific songs with tricky rhythm. He raised his eyebrows at her and said, "I saw what you can do to a beach house with a few rolls of toilet paper. I think you can handle whatever we throw at you." But then, he actually answered all her questions, and Geno joined in, too. By the time they got through her list, she felt reasonably sure she could handle it, too.

"You almost ready?" El said. He planted a kiss on her as naturally as if they'd been together forever. She heard a little "ooooooh" from behind her and knew it was Mikey making fun. And the difference forty-eight hours made was that she didn't care. She had a boyfriend. She had a band of friends. And no matter who was in the crowd or if she lost her timing for a moment, she knew she was exactly where she was supposed to be.

"Let's go!" she said. She jumped on the stage and threw her bass strap over her shoulder.

Dave was taking a long swallow of orange drink; he widened his eyes in signature form and gave her a thumbs up. Putting his cup down, he said, "We gotta take anyone out tonight?"

She grinned. "No, sir." Their queue-up song, "Sabotage," started to play. She shouted over the opening bars. "El and I took care of everything."

Jessie

THE FIFTH OF JULY CONTINUED. SAM, ALL alone, brought us breakfast he'd picked up in the apparent best place for it in Blairsville. After a few bites of fresh peaches and cream pancakes and crispy bacon, I was already sold out to the farm-to-table restaurant called The Sawmill Place. I mentally added it to our list for our next, hopefully less eventful trip, coming in just over a week. I didn't mention it to my groggy husband, who was enjoying his own stack of bacon and eggs, a grilled biscuit that I might have stolen a taste of, and hot sauce and grits with quiet enthusiasm. I knew he wouldn't argue.

Sam and I took to the front porch while Paul lay down for a nap. The sun was rising toward the noonday sky, heating up everything. Later, the kids would hopefully get to come splash in the creek again. We had contacted the cabin owner and managed to get it for one more night, and when she heard about our accident, she even waived the cleaning fee. We had already booked the cabin for a whole week later in the month, and at this point I was ready to volunteer as caretaker and stay there for the rest of the summer.

"Mama," Sam said, his gaze toward the babbling brook parallel to mine. "You and Paul don't have to come back for the move. It was already a lot to ask, and now with the… and everything…"

My heart warmed at how he just skipped any descriptive word of the last night's events. No "accident" or "incident" or "the thing with the Jeep and my kids" or anything. I wanted to reach over and squeeze him, but it would hurt me and probably irritate him, so I just cast a sidelong glance and gave thanks for my first best guy.

"Thank you," I said. "You didn't ask; we offered. And we want to come. I think we'll be just fine, but if we aren't recovered enough to be much physical help, maybe we will wait a few days. Or maybe we can keep Summer and Jacob at the beach for a few extra days, so you can—"

"Mama, they have to come with us," Sam said. I thought he was joking, because of course they had to go with their parents. But his face was solemn, even mournful.

"I wasn't going to steal them," I said, leading gently.

"Well, I know you want to," he said, a little lighter. "And I already don't know if we're doing the right thing. I already don't want to leave."

Ooch. Here was one of the things no one could ever teach you about parenting: how best to console your kid when you could barely console yourself. How could I convince him to be brave when I'd rather beg him to stay?

"Oh bud, aren't you just in love with this little town?"

I said, and I did mean it. "The kids will have a blast exploring all those shops. They'll be on a first-name basis with everyone on the square. And you and Abby can hike together. Look at how beautiful everything is. You'll stay busy getting to know a whole new university. And Travis will come visit, and so will we. It will be an adventure… just like when your dad and I moved to the beach."

He nodded. "And you never looked back."

I ticked off the years and memories and huge life events, including three additional children being added to our family, that had taken place after Randall and Sam and I moved to the beach. It was as though our life in Illinois had been a tiny blip, and our real life started in South Carolina. Sam was older now than we had been, but maybe that drove the point home ever further. He was able to navigate a new chapter with the wisdom only life experience could bring. And in the past two years, like the rest of us, he had learned perhaps the most important lesson of all:

"Nothing is forever," I said. "Nothing good gets to last forever, and nothing bad has to stay forever. So take stock of right now, what you have in this moment, and be grateful for it. Worrying about what comes next wastes all your energy. The only thing that is real is what and who is with you right now."

I waited a beat as he considered.

"Abby already seems happier," he said, nodding.

"She does," I agreed.

"And the kids are fine. Not just…I don't just mean from last night, although thank God, but in general. They'll adapt and they'll be exactly who they are, just in a new place."

"Yes, they will."

There was silence. The creek sounded so hypnotic I honestly could have fallen asleep. But the mountain air had a mystic heaviness to it between my son and me there on that porch. I knew he wasn't finished.

"And you are only down the road," he said, and at that moment, he reached over and took my hand.

"I am only down the road." I was still working hard to strike that balance of being encouraging and honest. "We've never been apart, Sam. I won't pretend it will be easy for me, and I can't help feeling just a little relieved that it won't be easy for you, either. But we are both equipped for this. Dad taught us how to be strong. And we picked the right people to carry on with, didn't we?"

He smiled. I let my eyes fill.

"This move would be so much harder if Paul wasn't there. It's not that you can't handle it, because I think you can do anything, but he makes you shine again. And he loves Kayla and Brit, too. Makes me feel less guilty."

"Please don't feel guilty." We both laughed. I, as recovering mom-guilt addict, had no room to talk.

"They're doing fireworks in the square tonight," Sam added. "I know our family never has to look far for fireworks, but maybe we can try again?"

"We'll rest awhile this afternoon," I said, looking out at the big yard. It was so lush and peaceful and so big, completely different from the one we had at home. But as soothing as the sound of the creek was, I was already missing the ocean being just a two-minute walk away from home – our home, my home with my new husband for our new life. I know he wanted to try the ice cream place in the square again; he and Jacob had made big plans.

I looked at Sam and nodded. "But for tonight, I know Paul will agree: we should definitely try again."

WATCH FOR MORE OF THE OAKLEY-JAMESON FAMILY ADVENTURES IN THE FORTHCOMING SURFSIDE BEACH SERIES NOVEL, *THE BEST OF THEM.*

AFTERWORD

I Feels Like Home

QUITE UNLIKE LIFE FOR MY OWN KIDS, I LIVED IN ONE PLACE FOR MY ENTIRE CHILD-HOOD. I stayed in the same school district. I graduated high school with people I sat next to on the red rug in kindergarten. My memories still contain landline phone numbers of the parents of some of those same friends, although literally none of them live where they used to. But for our growing up, it was one place, one home in the suburbs. We could walk to school, to each other's houses, to Kmart for the latest in *Sweet Valley High* or Harry's New Town for some saganaki or a virgin strawberry daquiri, the height of sophistication. We could walk to the video store, our jobs, and virtually any place we needed to in order to find trouble. And we could probably navigate those streets with our eyes closed.

Life for my kids is quite different. When my baby daughters were just three and four years old and their big sister was sixteen, we moved from south of Chicago to South Carolina, emphasis on *by the beach*. After 34 years in one place, the idea of *home* was firmly engrained in me. Home was where I couldn't go anywhere – not even to Wrigley Field – without running into someone I knew. *Home* was cold and gray from sometime in September to sometime in April, maybe May. Home never snowed when you wanted it to. Home was hopping on the express way to get to a friend's house across a few towns or for a ride into Chicago, which could take anywhere from thirty minutes to two hours. Home was the best little ice cream shop, the best *thin-crust* pizza (don't come at me with your clichés), the best little Mexican eateries with names like Burrito Station and Lucky Burrito, and the best morning news crew on WGN. Home was knowing that cousins of the first, second, and third degree, aunts and uncles, neighbors, teachers, the person you met at Vacation Bible School in 1989 or waited on at Marvell Bakery in 1993 might be in line next to you at "the Jewels."

Before we moved, we threw ourselves an *epic* "see youS later" party. I will never forget the feeling of it, as people from many walks of life came by to wish us well. I felt like I was on the old show "This Is Your Life," or at my own wedding reception. That night, I wept, telling my husband, "I will never have this again."

Obviously, I didn't know anything about moving – and I certainly didn't know what it means to enter a new life as an adult and put down roots in a place of one's own choosing.

That is what is truly epic.

Two-and-a-half years is what it took. Roughly, after that time, I could barely go anywhere in our smallish town without running into someone I knew from somewhere. In those first months, we met so many people through start-up business efforts (that, my friends, is a book unto itself), our church, and our kids' schools. And today, as I wrote this, we are coming up on 13 years here, and sometimes I feel like the mayor. It drives my kids crazy, but we've gotten entwined in a lot of communities here, and though Myrtle Beach/Surfside Beach/Murrells Inlet really is one of the fastest growing areas in the country, for those of us with roots here, it's still a small town.

(Actually, I am writing this at the real Benjamin's Bakery, and along with knowing the owner and many of the workers here by name, I have come across three other random people I know while sitting outside.)

When we moved to town, we knew *no one*. Our closest friends were two hours away. I fulfilled my Jessie-like need to be hospitable by baking treats for our friendly neighborhood ad agency (I am still friends with the owner there, too!) When it came time to fill out those emergency contact papers for my daughters' pre-school, I nearly had a meltdown before bashfully asking a few new church friends if I could use their numbers. And it's amazing, as life moves at the speed of light, how many times since I have been asked to do the same thing for others. "Yes, new mama in town. Put down my name and number! I gotchu!"

- One year after we moved to town, our oldest son and his then-girlfriend/now-wife followed.
- Six years after we moved to town, my parents finally cracked and came. In that same week, so did my husband's surrogate parents.
- My bonus kids' mom has moved here. My daughter-in-law's dad and stepmom and cousins have moved here.

I honestly don't know what everyone else is waiting for!

Oh, and we had another baby, which put us in a yet another demographic and community and added us to the category known as *Natives*. We aren't, but Jack Burton sure is!

All that said, it's hard these days to imagine anywhere else being home for us. I love these streets. I love being close to the beach. I love the laid-back ways of the coastal south. I love sweet tea and barbeque (that is pulled pork with vinegar-based sauce, not "random stuff you cook on the grill"), and seafood (though I have to stay away from those first two a good bit). I love the restaurants we frequent and all the proprietors we personally know. I love how there are festivals every weekend from April through October and live music everywhere. I love our home, and I also love running past Jessie and Paul's house (yes, it's real) and imagining that I might live in it someday.

And honestly, the home of my adulthood has given me an appreciation for nature that I never had before. Sure, you can be outside in the frozen tundra we call Illinois, but to me, it was mostly miserable. Here, I can't get enough of it. Sunshine. Sand. Salt. Even when it's cold, it's usually bright. Even when it's hot, the ocean is still *right there.* And even when it rains, it's either warm or *it doesn't last for weeks on end.*

So would we ever move?

Well, Florida does have Disney World. But truly, there is only one place that Rod and I muse about sometimes, and that is (can you guess?)—

Blairsville, Georgia.

We discovered Blairsville in 2019, when Rod found a motorcycle lodge there, and we took our first bona fide Harley trip. That story is now one of our favorites, how my husband is an amazing driver in those winding mountain roads, and how his wife who never sits still and does *nothing* kept falling asleep. (Luckily, I am lodged in that seat pretty darn good).

In 2020, when so much of the world was shut down – and many people were vacationing near our beach, because we were not – I found the cabin you read about in this story. The word "whimsical" was indeed used in its rental listing and was absolutely the truth. We have been back to Blairsville every year since, sometimes twice, and now we won't stay anywhere but at "our" cabin.

It's strange how much it feels like home there. We don't know a soul, and we barely know our way around, and there is definitely no beach. And yet… every time we pull up the road and make the little turn and see the little sign, my heart shouts "Yay!" even as my soul whispers "Peace." From those rocking chairs facing the creek to the firepit where we've gathered with our kids, our grandkids, and one amazing weekend (so far), just the two of us, from the perfectly rustic, mismatched dining set to the cozy bedrooms with all the quilts… I feel like our cabin is truly our home away from home, more so than where I came from, more than any other place I have visited, and even more than Main Street, Magic Kingdom (sorry, kids).

When we eat at The Sawmill Place or shop at Sunrise Grocery, I think people recognize us. And when we go to our favorite little shops and nooks and crannies, I feel like I recognize the people there. We have visited other little mountain towns these past few years and not had quite the same experience. So I don't know what it is about Blairsville, but it's ours. And the first time we rode our motorcycle through those winding mountain roads, I imagined who might live there, and thought about a woman from Chicagoland, one of Puerto Rican and Irish parentage, one who needed to find a new life in a new place, and that's when Van was born. She will have her own story one day, but for now, I am happy to include her and her family in Jessie's extended, gathered clan.

On that note, my final thought about what makes home… *home*: It's our people. It took me years, trial and error, and realizing I could not recreate what I left in Illinois before I found my South Carolina circle. Some of the people have come and gone, and that's okay, but some have become stuck like glue. They are the Maggie to my Jessie, the Brittney to my Katy, the Van to my Abby. We need those people. They are worth the wait. They make home… home.

…and so do our partners. Rod and I are at a point in life at which the kids' needs from us are evolving and even lessening by the day. We are starting to think about what that proverbial next act looks like, where it takes place, what we will do when we get there. My hope is it will include a whole lot of home – here, maybe there—and a whole lot of experiencing new places and things. But if I have learned anything during these adult years when everything can change in the blink of an eye, is that as long as we're together, it feels like home to me.

- Kelly
April 29, 2024

#SURFSIDEROCKS

LISTEN & STAY TUNED AT
THESALTYLIPS.COM

Another Fifth of July Playlist:

Carolina Comfort, Wahoo Creek
Don't Fence Me In, Bing Crosby
Give it Away, Red Hot Chili Peppers
Run, Collective Soul
Breath, Breaking Benjamin
The Middle, Jimmy Eats World
Better Man, Pearl Jam
El Cerrito Place, Kenny Chesney
You Belong with Me, Taylor Swift
Wildflowers, Tom Petty
Would, Alice in Chains
Sting, Fields of Gold
Roll with It, Steve Windwood
Boys of Summer, Don Henley(& also The Ataris)

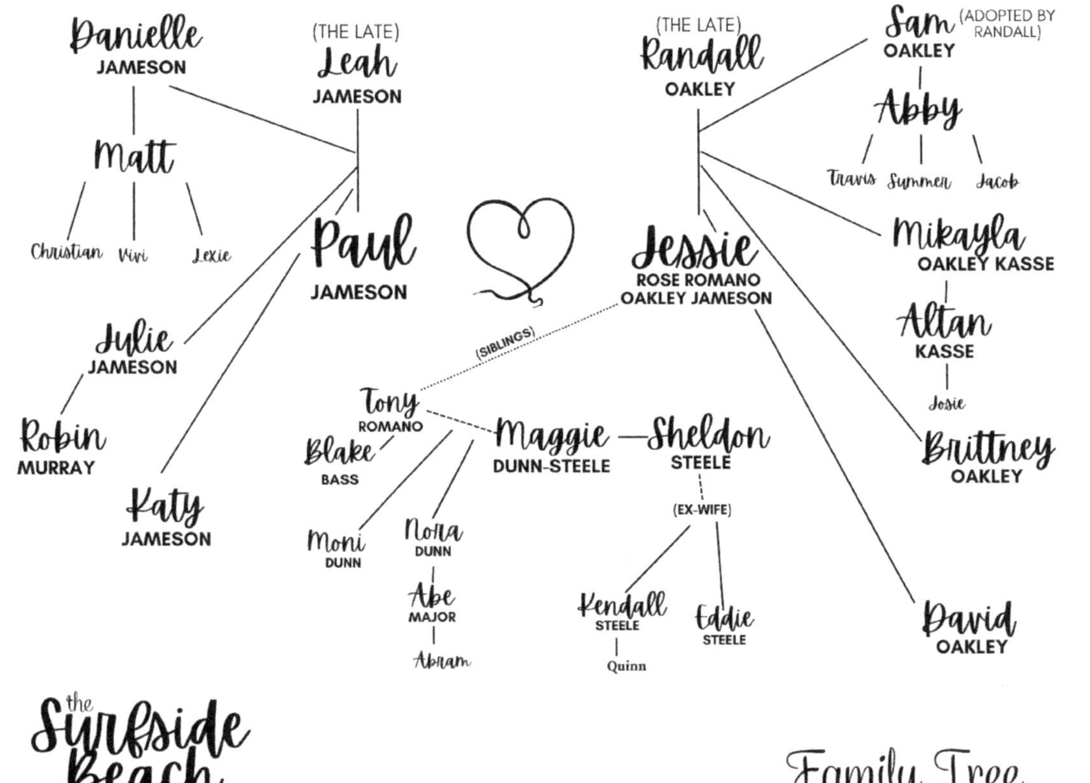

the Surfside Beach series
Family Tree
Danielle JAMESON
(THE LATE) Leah JAMESON
Matt
Christian Vivi Lexie
Paul JAMESON
Julie JAMESON
Robin MURRAY
Katy JAMESON
(SIBLINGS)
Tony ROMANO
Blake BASS
Moni DUNN
Nora DUNN
Abe MAJOR
Abram
Maggie DUNN-STEELE
Sheldon STEELE
(EX-WIFE)
Kendall STEELE
Quinn
Eddie STEELE
(THE LATE) Randall OAKLEY
Jessie ROSE ROMANO OAKLEY JAMESON
Sam OAKLEY (ADOPTED BY RANDALL)
Abby
Travis Summer Jacob
Mikayla OAKLEY KASSE
Altan KASSE
Josie
Brittney OAKLEY
David OAKLEY

SPECIAL THANKS TO:

Carla Hopkins and Melissa Dotson, my super efficient copy editors... Cheers to the south surburban girls!

Some real-life humans who grace my life and our lovely little locale and also appear on these pages: Dave Panzer, Deron Hunter of Jeremy's Ten and his lovely kiddos, Draven, Piper, Eva, and Vivien, Santa Greg and Nancy, Richard and Brenda Estep, and Ed "Fishwalk" Einhaus. *(The tavern isn't real, yet)*.

These amazing places that my family loves to frequent:
In Surfside Beach/Murrells Inlet, South Carolina: Benjamin's Bakery & Coffee Roasters, Neal & Pam's/Neal's Creekhouse, Painter's/Drippy's Ice Cream, and Mulberry Street NY Pizzeria. In Blairsville, Georgia: Sunrise Grocery, Jim's Smokin' Que, and The Sawmll Place. *(The tea room isn't real, yet!)*

My husband, Rod, who doesn't have to rise to the occasion of my whims and goals, because he is always standing up, either beside me or waiting for me. I love you, my best.

My miraculous kids, for the love, laughter, and endless possibilities you bring to me every day.

During the season of life when I was writing of this story, I was blessed, inspired, enlightened, and challenged by a special variety of friends, either in my everyday life or via an encounter at just the right time. Rather than overthink about all the names I need to include, I trust you know my heart and that you are in it! Thank you for your inspiration!

21 STORIES OF MESSY LIVES & AMAZING GRACE.

A NOTE FROM THE AUTHOR

THANK YOU FOR READING THIS FAR!
It's an uphill climb for independent authors to get their books into your hands, so however you found this one, I am grateful. If you enjoyed the story, you can help me more than I can express to you by leaving a review of this book on Goodreads, Amazon, and/or wherever you purchased it. Share it on your social media and tell your friends about it! And if you belong to a book club, get in touch with me! I love joining in your discussion, and sometimes, I even bring my own Maggie!

kcb@kellofastory
Instagram @kellofastory
Facebook @kellofastory